A·R· MEYERING

UNREAL CITY

A NOVEL

**INNISFREE
Press**

Cover, interior book design, and eBook design
by Blue Harvest Creative
www.blueharvestcreative.com

Editing provided by
BHC editor Bailey Karfelt

UNREAL CITY

Published by
Innisfree Press

ISBN-13: 978-0692313688
ISBN-10: 0692313680

Visit the author at:
Website: *www.armeyering.com*
Facebook: *www.facebook.com/AlexandraMeyering*
Twitter: *@ThatFairfaxGirl*
Goodreads: *www.goodreads.com/author/show/7753852.A_R_Meyering*

Purchase other books by A.R. Meyering in print, eBook, or audio by scanning the QR code.

To my brother,
for showing me the way

"That corpse you planted last year in your garden,
Has it begun to sprout? Will it bloom this year?
Or has the sudden frost disturbed its bed?"

~ Eliot, The Waste Land ~

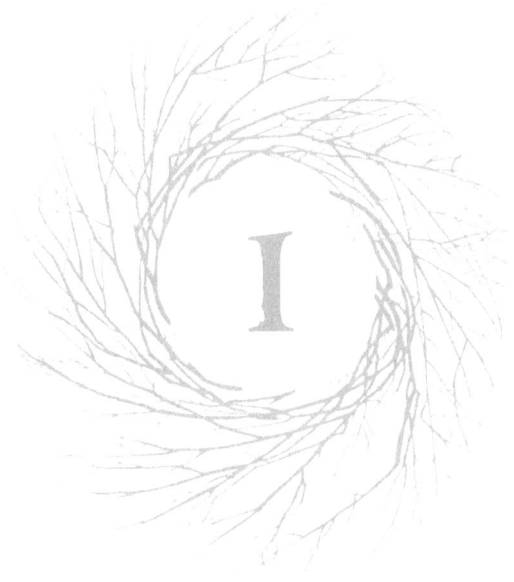

FOR THE REST of my life, no matter how I tried, I could not erase the image of that bed from my memory. There was nothing so terrible about the bed itself; the sheets were clean and neatly tucked under the sides of the mattress, and God knows I went on to see things that would haunt even the most hardened of souls, but it was that bed that always disturbed me the most. To me, the first time I opened the door to reveal it waiting in the gray confines of what was to become my dorm room, it represented everything I had lost. It was the space Lea had left behind after she died.

I dropped my suitcase when I saw it. I could almost hear her voice as I touched the fabric, a lump rising in my throat.

"I want the bottom bunk, Sarah. It'll be a pain to climb down every morning. Please?"

"Of course," I mumbled, talking to her even now, months after she'd faded from the world. Dutifully I made the choice that I would never sleep there. That I *could* never sleep there.

It was move in day on campus. The sound of excited college freshman, their voices shrill with nerves, roused me from my grief-induced stupor. Peering back, I received careful glances, weak smiles, and looks of panic hidden behind veils of composure. I knew it was just my imagination, but I couldn't find a single approachable face among all of them. I shut the door and hid.

In the space of a few hours I transformed the room. A homey touch here, a memory posted there. My familiar possessions were re-arranged into uncanny patterns, and by the time the cloud-shielded sun had sunk low behind the silhouettes of the pines, I was home — or inside some semblance of it. Yet even in the patchwork comfort that was my dorm room, the empty bed nagged at me. It was like Lea had been sitting there watching me unpack the whole time, quiet and smiling.

Looking around the filled-in living space, I took in my new territory. There were two desks pushed against opposite walls, one bare and one with a photograph of Lea and me with our parents beside my laptop. I straightened it, examining the image of our family before it had been fractured by death. My sister's face had been the mirror image of mine, our hair the exact same shade of pale blonde. In the photo my hair was its usual mess, hanging around my shoulders in unkempt waves, while Lea's was thick, straightened, and reached down almost to her waist. We had the same fair complexion, the same blue eyes — round and almost too big for our faces. Our noses matched perfectly, sharp and pointed above a square jaw. We had so obviously been twins. Even now, when I catch a quick glimpse of myself in a reflective surface, I think I'm seeing her.

A knock at the door disturbed me from my musing. I opened it to see another freshman girl with frizzy brown hair tied back into a ponytail and thick-framed black glasses staring at me. She flashed that same timorous smile we all wore.

"Hey," she greeted me. "We're having a little party. Just getting to know some of the people on our floor. You can—you can come if you like. I'm Kelly, by the way, um, what's—"

"Sarah." I anticipated her question and faced her blankly for a moment, deliberating whether I wanted to go and meet the other kids on my floor. It was an opportunity which seemed as harrowing as it did imperative. And I was afraid. I didn't like meeting new people on principle. I don't trust myself around them—I'm never sure what might slip out of my mouth.

Moving into college alone had seemed like a risk today, especially in light of what it had meant to Lea and I. But since the theme of the day seemed to be taking risks, I decided this was a promising idea. "Sure," I said. "Sounds like fun."

"Good! This way. We're over here…I think." Kelly led me uncertainly down the hall and into a room.

The college I had been placed in was called Merrill, one of many that made up the vast campus. According to the website they're a "close-knit bunch". As we stepped into the smoky dorm room to see it packed full of strangers getting better acquainted with one another, I knew the website was spot-on. I saw all the usual suspects: three boys with shaggy hair passing around a pipe that was choking the room with a heady, skunk-like odor, a girl with short-cropped hair engaged in vigorous conversation about her strict vegan diet, a pock-marked young man joking loudly about obscene subjects for a girl's attention. They all looked over as Kelly and I entered the room. Some of them put up their hands in a half-hearted wave. Names were exchanged, and I only caught a few of them. Jason, Samantha, Claire, Dean.

We recycled the same tired topics. Favorite bands. Home-towns. What made us *special*. I tried to relax as I made conversation, still watching myself closely, keeping my answers safe. After only an hour we were all laughing together like old buddies. The loud boy—Dean—actually had a pretty sharp sense of humor underneath his token vulgarities, and I suppose I inhaled enough of the smoke floating around in the air to make even those seem hysterical.

Unfortunately we arrived at the unavoidable question: "So what's everyone's major?"

Though my smile didn't fade, I felt my heart sink. I was still undecided. Hell, most freshmen are, but something about admitting it always made me uncomfortable. *Undefined.* The world expects direction from us at this age, I suppose. Pressure always made it hard for me to commit to anything. I lied and said photojournalism, which was something I was a part of in high school. I knew enough to bullshit about it. Tennis and photography were what had consumed most of my life in my last year of high school. I'd made a bunch of close friends through those activities. Before summer, anyway. The only friend I had left now—and to call her that was stretching it—had driven me here today on her way up to San Francisco. She'd left me in front of my dorm with a dispassionate farewell, as if we were only acquaintances. *Best friends forever.* It never ceases to amaze me how fragile those forevers turn out to be.

We were all starting to get caught up in the haze of the night, nobody really wanting to stay but nobody strong enough yet to be alone in this new place. The smoke was getting heavier and I decided to share a few puffs. Even after Lea's death I'd never fallen far into the world of *responsible* substance abuse, though I regarded it with curious neutrality. If it's there, why not? When she was still around, it was a different story. But as my head grew foggier, I became quiet with the heaviness of memories, something that Dean noticed as I became more absent from the conversation.

"What's-a-matter with you, Sarah? Miss your mom already?" There was a desperation in his humorous tone; he wanted me to admit it so that everyone else could have permission to break down too. However, my guard went up. I wouldn't allow him the pleasure at my expense.

"Not really," I snapped.

"What's up, then? You seem kinda off all of a sudden."

"Nothing. I'm tired. Move in day, and all." My hand flitted to the pendant that always hung around my neck, an unconscious motion of protection. He shrugged and they went back to their revelry, but my sense of ease had been disrupted.

Jason grabbed Dean's guitar from the corner of the room and started fiddling around on it and swaying to the music. Dean's eyes glowed with proud ownership of the instrument and he launched into the details of the fine piece of workmanship. In his own world, Jason started hammering out a Nirvana song and singing loudly over him. The other kids joined in. Goaded by their enthusiasm, Jason swung around the guitar like he was onstage at a rock concert. The neck came close to the corner of the desk, and Dean stood up to seize it.

"Dude, watch out. If you break that thing, I'll murder you and hide your body in the woods."

I was on my feet before I realized what I was doing, my cheeks hot with rage. "That's not fucking funny, asshole. Murder is not a joke," I shouted, my finger extended in an accusatory gesture. I hated myself for being unable to stop this emotional reaction. "Someone back me up here!"

The atmosphere turned uncomfortable as all eyes fixed on me and then I was charging out of the room with my tail between my legs. Their faces had been confused, hurt, and even concerned, but I still felt as if I were under attack. Making a great reputation for myself from day one was my specialty.

Aching with shame and furious at myself, I rushed back to my room and sat down at my desk in a huff. I had become the person that my friends and I used to mock. The ones who we were polite to when they were around, but constructed cruel inside jokes about when they were not.

I tried to get my mind off it, but social media offered no distraction and I closed the browser almost as soon as I opened it. I stared blankly at the desktop — another photo of Lea and me, this time on the boardwalk at home, in Monterey. We used to walk there after school sometimes. It had been one of those hazy, late afternoons and the sun backed us, the shadow making it difficult to tell who was who. I gazed at the photo for a long time, then took my computer to bed with me, clicked into a folder containing different shots I had taken over the years, and fell into the slideshow. The good times illuminated the screen and faded away, each one bringing a bittersweet feeling in my chest.

Photography interests me for different reasons than why I think most people get into it. A lot of them do it for the art of the process and result. I do it for the nostalgia. There's something supremely safe about a frozen moment. Something that ensures it never truly disappears. I like to collect such moments, keep them preserved, and enjoy them again and again. It's almost proof that the love shared between the people in the photo was real, at least for an instant.

And that was the comfort I sought on my first night. I revisited Lea, her entire story already told in eighteen short years of life. Memories of trips to Disneyland came back. Nights of silliness when she, her boyfriend, and I had talked until three in the morning. Our sixteenth birthday party. Halloween when we were little girls — Lea dressed in the likeness of a fairy and me as a rabbit. Lea kissing Fenris, our old gnarled Husky dog, on the side of the head. Every time I got sleepy and closed my eyes for a bit, they would flutter open just to make sure the photos hadn't gone away.

I fell asleep with little trouble, as I always do, though that night the rarity that was a dream came to me. I hardly ever remember my dreams, and when I do it's usually vague, colorless images or general feelings. But that night I dreamt I was standing at the edge of a pier, high above the water. Dark, mammoth shapes were circling the pier and disturbing the already choppy waves. I had a feeling that they would jump up toward me soon, but just as I saw a rising body of slick, leathery flesh, I woke, disoriented and confused about where I was.

Then I remembered and my head returned to my pillow. I stared at the shapes of the trees through the cracks in the blinds as I drifted back to sleep, and thought I saw a shadow slink past the dim blueness of the hours before dawn. It stirred me for a moment, but I reminded myself that the campus was built in the middle of a redwood forest. The animals had been here first. They hadn't up and left just because humans planted a school there. I had already seen two deer on my walk to the Merrill dorm. Since I was on the ground floor, I knew I'd probably have to get used to seeing a parade of fauna pass by my window every night.

Now that I look back on it, I probably should have had the good sense to be more afraid. If I had been even a bit more alert, I might have taken more notice of a weird, atonal tune whining through the wind. But I was a different person then, unassuming of dark things, blissfully unaware, even secure in the belief that the worst that could ever happen to me had already come and gone, leaving behind a hell of an aftermath to sort through.

But maybe that's also why I like photos. You can *see* the innocence in people's faces and look back on them in melancholy hindsight. They never have any idea of what's coming for them, do they?

2

MOST OF THE time before I went down into the Caves
is a blur to me now. School started and we were force-fed a
more-than-healthy portion of rules and regulations. I rushed
around the massive campus desperately trying to catch buses,
but mostly getting lost in the miles of forest.

I remember a sense of wonder at the campus itself. Mists
curling in and out of the massive redwoods and sprawling
ferns could be seen almost everywhere during early mornings
and late evenings, and sometimes they rolled in during the day.
Getting stuck in the middle of one of those walls of fog while
on the way to class felt like being in a different world. Sometimes I'd pass another lonely student in the grayness, make
eye contact for a mere moment, and glance back to see them
disappear into the mist as if they were the last person I was
ever going to see. Dew-beaded webs decorated every clearing
and spiders, fat and bright green, hung heavy on their surfaces
like bulbs on a Christmas tree.

I got a sense of everything *growing* around me, of plants
moving in and consuming the buildings that invaders had

dared to construct. I stumbled across many wonderful and enchanting places on my first weeks while hiking in the September heat that so easily transformed into rain. I don't know how I found it, but there was a lovely little garden tucked away somewhere that I happened upon once and couldn't relocate, no matter how long I searched.

The thing that interested me most, and that I actively sought, was something the other students called the Wishing Tree. They said that if you wrote your wish down on a paper and left it on the tree, it was sure to come true. Something about that stirred my numbed heart, and the first weekend I took the time to go on a little journey to see it for myself. Sure enough, it was already covered in rain-bleared wishes, but instead of exciting me the way I had hoped it would, my heart ached at the sight of it. My eyes fell on the dreams of my classmates: *"Please get Jordan to ask me out"*, *"Let me do well this quarter"*, *"I wish for people to stop hating one another"*. I felt like an intruder. I'd brought paper with me and tried to think of a wish on the way through the meadow, but after standing there for a minute I just folded it up, stowed it in my bag, and stared at the branches.

"I wish I could go back to being me," I told the tree, then shoved my hands into my pockets and turned back for Merrill College.

The first warning that things were not right came one evening as I was on the way back from my Intro to Sociology class. It was after nightfall, and the day had gone from T-shirt weather to a wind so biting I wished I'd thought of bringing a coat. I was crossing one of the long, wooden bridges built at an uncomfortable height above chasms brimming with plant life, and my mind was fixed on how much I did not want to go through with the group project my class had been assigned.

Suddenly, I saw what looked like a face staring at me from the gulch. I stopped walking and leaned forward to get a closer look. The bushes shivered and the ghost-green flash of an animal's eyes glinted as the black, shaggy shape of what looked like a bobcat leapt out and skittered away. Seeing so many animals on campus was still unusual for me.

When I arrived back at the dorm, my phone buzzed and I answered it to hear the voice of my mother. It made me want to cry; I was homesick despite my constant denials.

"Sarah! How are things? We hardly hear from you—I wanted to give you your space, but Dad and I are getting curious and—"

"Mom, it's good to hear from you. Things are—well, they're really good, actually." I caught myself smiling as I tossed my bag aside and plopped into the desk chair, the feeling of eeriness I'd gotten from seeing the bobcat already washed away. "Though I have to admit it's getting a bit lonely. I miss you guys. How're things back at the homestead?"

"Oh, nothing's changed." I couldn't help but notice Mom sounded really tired. "Things are busy, busy, busy. Book club, sewing circle, painting, keeping up with friends—oh, and I started taking a Wine Studies class! We're both college kids now, isn't that funny?"

I faked a laugh.

Ever since the day we'd gotten the call about Lea, my mother had refused to sit still for a minute. She arranged the funeral and dealt with all the finances alone while Dad and I tried to hold ourselves together. It disturbed me how frantic she was about filling her life with activity, because I knew how terrified she was of being alone. But she still wept. We all did, only she would do it when she thought no one could hear her, and it broke my heart again and again to see the way she'd hastily wipe tears away, stifle wails, and force the ugliest smile I've ever seen when I came to check on her.

It had affected us all differently. My father's safe-haven became his routine, and if anything altered it I'd see an angrier side of him than I ever had before. It disgusted me to realize that Lea had taken so much of what I loved about my family and myself with her. It disgusted me that I thought she was selfish for doing so, but I did all the same.

We chatted for a while about safe subjects like my classes, new friends, and anecdotal incidents that had happened in class, but when there came a long, pregnant pause, I knew what was coming. The answer to a question that had been in the back of my mind since my phone had rung, but I had been too afraid to ask.

"Nothing's changed with Stephen. The doctors say there's almost no sign of brain activity and they have no clue when he might wake up. Actually, they're not sure he'll wake up at all at this point. But his parents are doing everything they can. No one's given up hope just yet," Mom said in a flat voice.

I made a low noise to show I'd heard her, but didn't respond. Stephen had been Lea's boyfriend, and they'd found him next to her body on the night she died, along with another boy from our high school. Lea and the other boy, Isaac, had been murdered. Stephen was still alive, but only just. He had remained almost untouched, except for a cut on his hand and innocuous scratches he'd likely gotten as he fell to the ground; yet ever since that day, he'd remained in a coma.

Isaac and Lea were found in the exact same condition: both had drowned to death. People drown all the time at the ocean. Accidents happen. But we knew it couldn't have been an accident—all three of them were found in the center of the town, miles away from the beach. I hated to even imagine what had transpired. Had someone held her down and forced water down her throat until she died? Had she been awake while it happened? How badly had it hurt? Was the sick fuck who had done it just getting his kicks by watching her and the other kid gasp for air as they slipped away?

I'd always heard of these things happening, like in those crime shows on TV where they expound upon the heinous acts of some psychopath. That kind of show just seems like a horror movie when you've lived a life untouched by evil. I couldn't imagine anyone wanting to hurt Lea. I've never met anyone who loved people more unconditionally than she did. That kind of stain inside of my mind — just knowing that somewhere in my hometown there had walked a person so cruel — a person that had taken my sister from me — that sort of feeling doesn't dissipate with time. Once you find out just how real it is, you're never the same again.

But we'd never know what really happened until Stephen woke up. He'd seen it all; he must have. He'd know why there were no signs of a struggle. He'd know why they couldn't find a trace of any drug in any of their bodies during the autopsy.

The autopsy. Strangers had cut her up, butchered her, mutilated my sister with a scalpel, probing for the method used to strangle the life out of her and —

"Sarah, are you there?" My mother's voice fanned away the dark cloud that had been forming in my mind.

"Yeah, yeah...I'm just thinking about — I'm fine."

"Sarah, I was wondering...You know, maybe it wouldn't be a bad idea if, well, the school's got these great trained professionals, people that can help with —" Mom ventured, but I cut her off, anger rising into my throat.

"I'm not going to see a shrink. I'm not crazy, and I'm not going to pay anybody to be my friend and listen to me boohoo about how shitty my life is!"

"Baby, we're worried about you. You don't need to be crazy to see a counselor, and many of them don't even charge. Maybe you can just check out the options and —"

"Mom, I've got to go. I just remembered I have a homework thing due tomorrow and I have to get working on it now. Sorry." I pulled the phone away from my ear, ignoring my mother's protests that tomorrow was Saturday, and ended the call. Knowing she would try to call back, I shut my phone off and grabbed my shower caddy and flip-flops.

The hot water did its job of easing the ache inside of me. I liked the feeling of making it just a little too hot, of feeling it burn my skin, all the while imagining it might be able to burn away some of the grief inside me. Cook it out, or something.

As I blow-dried my hair and stared at my reflection in the steamy mirror, I thought of mornings when Lea and I did this together. When we were little girls, my dad told us that when we took showers, if we wrote a wish of what we hoped would happen that day in the moisture on the glass and watch it as it disappeared, it had a pretty good chance of coming true. There were rules, of course—we couldn't wish for anything too big or use it too often, because it might screw with the signals or dry up the well, he claimed.

For years, Lea and I kept up that tradition. Many a math test was passed that way; many a secretly coveted Christmas gift obtained. As we got older, we did it less and less, or we did it with only humor in mind...but one day back in May, as we'd waited for our acceptance letters to come—God, she'd been alive then—Lea had gotten quiet just as the fog started to fade. She'd walked right up to the glass like it had only been yesterday that we believed in this, and wrote *I want to go to college with my sister* with her index finger. I smiled, almost walked out with a half-hearted laugh in my throat, then decided to wait and watch it fade. We got the emails that afternoon, but her wish had never come true.

The pain burst out from inside me like a train rampaging out of a tunnel. I crumpled to my knees, making a sound like an animal as the hairdryer clattered to the ground. I didn't care that I was in a public shower. I didn't care how filthy the ground was. The monstrosity that was my grief had risen up out of the cave it hid in to assail me again. It constricted my shoulders and ribs, forcing me to breathe in little wounded gasps as my face burned and tears flowed down my cheeks.

Give her back, give her back, please God, please...please let me have her back. I don't want to go through this life without her.

I sobbed on the grimy, watery ground, curling into a fetal position and shivering there until I heard the door open. Not wanting to see who'd come in, I staggered to my feet, arms clutching my sides as I bolted from the bathroom with my head down. Back in my room, I climbed into my bed. Still choking back sobs, I took a firm grip on the pendant of my necklace, dug deep under the covers, and concealed myself within the safety of sleep.

I awoke almost thirteen hours later, feeling dizzy and unfocused. It was still early—a little after eight, and I was due to meet my partner for the group project at noon outside her dorm at Porter College. I decided I'd skip the unappetizing breakfast they offered at the dining hall, and in a last-ditch effort to get myself feeling better, I got my tennis stuff out of my closet, pulled my hair back into a messy ponytail, and made for the court.

There's nothing like hurling balls at the wall and smacking the living daylights out of them to relieve a little frustration. It was one of those chilly, dewy mornings that set the ferns and redwoods glimmering with moisture in the weak yellow glow. The air bit at me, raising gooseflesh on my arms and numbing the tip of my nose, but I liked it. I liked anything that got my blood flowing. The walk to the courts was a long one, and it gave me some time to clear my head. By the time I was swinging my racket with all my might and getting a few good volleys going, I was almost feeling like my old self. It was those kinds of instances that I lived for now: the rare hours of my day that felt like intermittent gasps of fresh air while being trapped in a stuffy cupboard. It didn't last long.

My flow was disrupted when one of my tennis balls shot off the board in a neon streak and bounced right over the fence and into the woods beyond. I made a frustrated clicking noise with my tongue and stared in the direction it had launched, wondering whether it was worth the effort to go hunting after it or just let it be taken by the woods. Deciding I was too caught up in my exercise to stop, I had fished another ball out of the tube and was preparing to lob it when a flash of fluorescent yellow came into my peripheral vision. My heart kicked up a little as I turned to see the lost ball bouncing toward me in little skips. It had come back to me.

Confused, I gazed into the trees bordering the court. No one was there. I picked up the ball and was surprised to feel warm dampness. My nose wrinkled and I dropped it, wiping the slime onto my shorts. The courts were deserted, and the only people in sight were running around the jogging track, farther than the average arm could throw. Taking a cautionary step forward, I felt my pulse rising as I peered further into the trees.

"Is…is someone there?" I called, my voice trembling despite how hard I tried to sound calm. Silence. I took a few more steps toward the fence and squinted to see if I could spot anything.

A foreboding feeling hit me in an instant. There was something threatening in those trees, something that *really* wanted me to come curiously peeking in. There was no reason for that thought, but it snuck up on me all the same and my chest tightened. The hairs on the back of my neck prickling, I retreated a few feet without really meaning to move. I told myself I was being stupid, but all the same there was an alarm going off in my head that was too loud to ignore.

Get outta here, Sarah. Now.

I've never been one for believing in premonitions or superstitions or dark intuitions of any kind, but that morning I listened to my gut. I left before I'd even gotten my blood running warm enough to negate the chill in the air. The dining hall with all its safety in numbers seemed pretty attractive all of a sudden. Seated at a table, I mechanically chewed an apple down to the core and waited for noon to come.

ON THE WINDING walk to Porter college I encountered a rusted metal merry-go-round for students. That was this university in a nutshell — a worn-out, rusted, lonely playground amid towers erected in the name of higher learning. It was still early, so I got on it and spun for a minute, watching three big words someone had painted on the inside canopy whirl by over and over again as my stomach fluttered pleasantly: *Seek your bliss. Seek your bliss. Seek your bliss.*

I made it to Porter and found my partner, Joy Sasaki, waiting outside her dorm for me. My nerves made me jumpy as I approached. Joy was a freshman like me. I'd liked her from the moment the teacher had briefly entwined our destinies together for the project. She had smiled warmly and approached without shyness. Her manner showed none of the dismal, eye-averting, forced politeness that I expected from classmates. She was a plain girl made beautiful by the kindness and warmth that shone on her face. Spotting me now she broke into a trademark, ear-to-ear smile. Her eyes were as dark as ink and lit up when she looked at people.

Joy welcomed me and led me inside to her dorm room, offering me a seat near her bed as her long hair rustled around her round face. On the other end of the room, her roommate sat on a bed with headphones on, engrossed in a laptop. I didn't bother to wave hello. The wall beside Joy's bed was covered with pencil sketches: figure drawings, still life, and detailed landscapes, all creating a little window into the imagination of an artist.

"Did you draw all of these?" I asked, admiring a beautiful rendition of a woman's back next to a bowl of fruit.

Joy's cheeks tinged with a rosy color and her smile broadened. "Yeah," she said, watching me scrutinizing her work anxiously.

The brilliance of the drawings was certainly in the precision and excellent proportions, but something in them lacked spirit, or life. I couldn't imagine anyone being unimpressed with her work, though, and I told her so. Joy appeared delighted by my little throwaway compliment and bounced into her computer chair. Her computer was covered in cute little stickers of cartoon animals, strawberries, and cupcakes. I grinned in spite of myself.

"Okay, so do you have any ideas for the project?" she asked and before I could even finish shrugging, piped up again, "'Cause I think I have a pretty good one. You know how society has had this shift where instead of avoiding things that make us afraid, we've produced an industry centered on them? Think about it: billion dollar horror movies, Halloween scare mazes, television shows designed to terrify us about the end of the world. The list goes on. What has changed in our world that has made us crave fear? Why do we spend so much effort and money looking for something to scare us? Does that sound like a good springboard topic?"

Her enthusiasm was obvious and since I couldn't care less, I nodded. Joy was pleased—it didn't seem to take much to achieve that with her—and we got to work on our Internet research. She was a good person to work with, and she made conversation easy, which relieved me.

These days, communicating with people seemed more like a battle than it ever had. I found it hard to think of things to say, and found it even harder to care about what others had to say. But something about Joy's charisma made it hard to react to anything she said with disdain. These past few months, I had grown used to feeling like I was constantly walking around with a huge, heavy sign around my neck that read: *My sister is dead. Please, for the love of God, will somebody feel sorry for me?*

I felt like everyone could read it, like they all instantly knew it just by glancing at me as I walked by. And I always felt like people would pointedly ignore the plea written on it. But it seemed that Joy could see it too, and instead of ignoring it she tried to help in her own way. Gently, of course. None of those precise yet meaningless platitudes that constantly pester those who have been stricken by grief. She spoke softly, paid careful attention when I said things, and seemed to genuinely care what I had to say. Her sensitivity was refreshing. We took a break from research and made small talk, and of course my favorite question came around.

"So, what's your major?"

"Photography." Lying came so easily when I wanted to avoid things. I didn't expect her to pursue it, but she did.

"Ooh, that's really cool. Got any pictures you've taken on your laptop? I'd like to see some, if you don't mind," she requested with those dark, bright eyes fixed on me.

I stared at her, wanting to refuse but feeling unable to quash her kindness. "Sure," I acquiesced after a moment, opening up a folder and turning my computer around for her to consider. I clicked through some pictures I'd taken in Monterey of the beach and various images of sea life, swimsuit-clad vacationers, and sunsets. A sick feeling washed over me as a photo I had taken of Lea and Stephen at prom filled the screen.

"Oh, you used to have long hair?" she asked amiably, and I hesitated before I shook my head, wondering how best to stop this conversation before it began. "Then —"

"That's my sister. We were twins." Past tense. Why did I use past tense? Now a question even better than *What's your major?* would come next. Joy stopped talking, her expression showing she was unsure how to voice her curiosity, so I decided to skip the awkwardness and cut to the chase.

"She died a few months ago. She was murdered," I said, hoping we could leave it there.

Joy's face darkened and she looked at me directly, trying to make eye contact. I refused to meet her gaze.

"Sarah…I'm so sorry. I—I had no idea, if—if there's anything I can do, or…I'm not sure if you wanna talk to someone about it, or…"

Her words came from an authentic place of sympathy and caught me off-guard. I was so unaccustomed to anyone daring to breach the unspoken grief-code of complete avoidance of the topic that I was rendered vulnerable. And when I feel vulnerable, I almost always defer to anger.

"Yeah, I'm fine. Don't worry about me," I snapped, and Joy recoiled. Guilt gripped me seconds after I'd spoken, and I cast my eyes to the corner of the room, gripping my pant leg as I waited for the discomfort of the moment to pass.

Joy's head dropped a little. "I apologize, I didn't mean to pry, or bring up bad memories…I just wanted to make sure that you were okay," she apologized. Her kindness made me hate myself even more, and I felt my anger bubbling up again, like stomach acid rising in my throat.

"'Okay?' Why do people always ask that stupid question? Like I'll just wake up one day and everything will be back to normal?" My voice rose with every word, and the angrier and more embarrassed I got, the more I felt myself wanting to attack her verbally. "I'm never going to be *okay* again. Never. How dare—" I bit my tongue hard to stop myself, tears stinging at the corners of my eye.

"I'm—I'm sorry, Joy, I—I'd better go. I didn't mean to. I'm sorry." I grabbed my laptop, shoved it into my bag, and fled from her dorm room and across the courtyard, past some people strumming on a ukulele. Their carefree happiness made my stomach churn, and I pushed past a massive, crimson, abstract sculpture.

Looking around for somewhere to go with my fury and shame still rising, I saw the trees at the edge of the meadow and bolted for them. I hated everything at that moment, but I urged myself to keep going. One foot. Then the other.

I tried to keep from breaking into an all-out run, my heavy messenger bag slamming rhythmically into my thigh as I descended the sloping meadow. The morning wind had died down; the grass was dry from the heat of the September afternoon and the ground hard and dusty. I batted at bees buzzing in my ears as I drew closer to the line of trees. The air here was sharp and clear, but it smelled heavily of pine, fertilizer, and dry grass.

I remember taking deep, heavy breaths of the layers of scents while crossing the brush of the meadow toward the trees. The closer I got to the edge of it, the more the sense of being drawn into the pines intensified. In there it was shady. It was cool. In there it was safe. The trees almost wanted me to wander in, come into the shadows, to the light-falls that shone in points of dappled clarity on the forest floors, to the disordered kingdom of humming insects, to the place where everything was simultaneously growing and dying at each other's hand. In those trees I could hear peace calling. I could hear something beckoning, offering a way to pierce my anger and rip it out, leaving me neutralized but tranquil.

Tormented by my jumble of furious, desperate thoughts and yearnings, I made it into the row of pines and away from the eyes of the world. Though there was a view of the freeway from here, it was quiet at last. The sun's rays didn't beat down quite as intensely while I was hiding in those woods. I took a moment to catch my breath and let my gaze fall to my shoes, so caught up in lamenting how poorly I had treated Joy that I became oblivious to the danger nearby. I didn't have an inkling that I was being watched until I glanced up to see the heart-stopping, unearthly face of a creature I then had no name for.

That was the first time I lay eyes on the nightmare that I would come to know so well.

3

I YELPED. I couldn't help it. That instant was like those moments in dreams when you realize everything around you is a façade, except I knew that it wouldn't fade like a dream—what I was seeing was real.

At the end of the narrow dirt trail sat a black-furred animal a little larger than a fox. I thought at first glance that it was a rather large cat, but its face proved me wrong. Those eyes were too bright and fiery green in color...and too *aware*. They were intelligent, sentient, and curious. Its skull was misshapen too, with a toothy mouth that curved up at a terrifying angle in an unmistakable grin. Its ears twitched slightly as it regarded me, those little needle teeth glinting all around its dark lips. It struck me then why the creature's face disturbed me so: it looked *human* almost—a hideous crossbreed of primal, animalistic rawness and human understanding.

In my horror, my foot slipped on the loose earth of the hill and I almost slid down the slope, causing my heart to pound even harder. My hand shot to my forehead as my vision refocused. That *thing* was really there. No matter how many times I blinked, it stayed there.

Terrified yet mesmerized, I stared at that ethereal abomination as it did the same to me — that mocking, dangerous grin still stuck to its face. Then without warning, with all the grace of a feline and more, it turned its bushy tail, skittered down the path, and was gone. I watched it go, my heart slamming against my ribcage.

What the fuck was *that?*

I wanted to leave, to run away from that unnatural, ungodly thing, but I couldn't. I don't think anyone could have. How could I continue on as if *that* hadn't just happened?

It took me a good long while to take a single step down the path where it had disappeared. But after that gargantuan effort of courage had been taken, the steps that followed came with rising momentum. I remained terrified as I hurried around the narrow bend on the forest path after the creature, but I needed to know. I needed to at least see it once more, to ensure that it *had* in fact been real.

The dirt trail began to slope downward to a little clearing. In the gulch below sat a large cement box with a square hole cut into it. I was just in time to see a little tuft of black fur disappear down into that hole. I knew what this place was. I'd heard the other students talk about it: Porter Caves.

All too aware of my recklessness, I slid down the sandy slope and climbed with shaking legs onto the box. I could see the edge of a rickety metallic ladder dropping down into the dark, but even after just a few feet, I could see nothing but darkness so deep that anything below it seemed to have disappeared from the Earth altogether.

"He-hello? Are you — is anything down there?" I'd meant to say *anyone* but it came out wrong. I waited, listening to the drumbeat of blood smashing rhythmically in my ears. There was no reply.

The idea of climbing down that ladder on a cheerful day would've seemed daunting. I won't pretend that it didn't take me quite some time to pluck up the courage to peer deeper into the hole. I was stuck. It was the feeling of being so averted to an inevitable future, coupled with a sick, fascinated yearning in the pit of my stomach. As I sat there, getting queasier by the minute, I just knew that whatever was down there was the same creature that had been hiding in the trees this morning. I felt that same sense of a looming, unnamed threat. It was the thing that had thrown me the tennis ball—like it had been fishing for me.

As anticipated, my fear gave way to anger and I threw my leg over the edge and began the descent into the dark. Halfway down, I fished my phone out of my pocket and turned on the camera flash to shine a feeble light down into all that dark. It came as a shock when the ladder turned flat and ran across the ground, and I stumbled with a little yelp, half-expecting something to start snapping at my sneakers.

Shaking from head to toe, I at last hit the bare bottom of the cave. The chunk of light from the world above seemed too far above my head to keep up any illusion of safety. I turned around slowly, gasping in a lungful of the stuffy air. It smelled of dank earth and marijuana, increasing my nausea.

"I saw you come in here. Where are you?" I tried to shout, but it came out in a pathetic whisper. I raised my phone with my shaking, grimy hand. Webby black plants that looked like veins hung from the cave ceiling and bits of discarded garbage floated around in the shallow, filthy pools of cave water.

I turned in a complete circle, and my shoulders slumped. *It's gone. How could it just be —*

My phone light fell on a crevice to the side of the ladder, and I caught a glint of green. The cave went deeper. Balling up my fists and gritting my teeth, I approached the narrow passage that led deeper into the cold, moist earth on uncertain legs.

"Come on out, you little shit. I know you're there," I snarled with a confidence I didn't feel.

The way down was tight and slimy, caking my hands and jeans in grimy clay. As I shone my tiny circle of light ahead, it caught the edge of a black, bat-like ear. There it was.

I screamed, feeling my panic spike. I couldn't get out; I was stuck down here with it and *I couldn't get out*. I scrambled up the rocky slope and slammed my knee into the stone. It hurt so bad that I wanted to double over, but I needed to get away — it was just too damn close. When I turned back, sprawled on my back and trembling like a leaf in the wind, it was still there. It put an experimental, black paw forward and cocked its head at me, as if my terror confused it.

"Wh-what *are* you?" I demanded, my teeth chattering.

It answered me with unwavering composure, its voice echoing inside my skull. "Hungry."

An awful thrill shot through me, as if I'd been injected with poison that swept through my veins with every frantic pump of my heart. I braced my back against the cave wall, getting as far away from the creature as I could. I was too scared to run, too scared it would chase me.

"Are you gonna eat *me*?" I breathed.

"Not unless you ask me to," it replied conversationally, yet with a hint of sadistic playfulness. There was no doubt in my mind he meant it. The creature — *demon* was the word I was thinking at that moment — laughed at me. His mouth never moved when he spoke or chuckled, but I heard it all the same, as if the intention was beaming into me like a laser.

It was as if in that moment a window of fogged glass had shattered and revealed an entire world beyond everything I had thought to be true. And it wasn't beautiful. It was petrifying. I wasn't ready; no one could be. It's easy to sit there and say you'd be ready to abandon the laws that dictate your world in lieu of something more exciting or fantastic, but when you're faced with it, I know from experience you'd give anything to go back to that safety. That ignorant time before the shift became a comfort that I longed for — that I *burned* for, like a parched throat in the desert.

I stared as he blinked those eyes that looked so much like gemstones backlit by a flame. "Forgive my glibness. I know I shouldn't tease," he apologized.

My shivering hand drew the light away from him for just a moment, and when I lifted it he was gone. The bottom of my stomach dropped out as I searched frantically around for him in the crevices, until a tickle of whiskers on the back of my neck signaled that he was right behind me. I cried out, the sound bouncing off the walls as I shuffled backward, deeper into the cave. His smile broadened, amused by my reaction.

"I am a familiar spirit, and I'm here to serve you, Sarah Wilkes."

My mouth went dry. "How do you know my name?"

"I've known you for a while, now. I've been around almost always, and I've heard your name from many mouths," the familiar said, padding silently closer to me with those terrible eyes glinting from the light of my phone. His eyes hurt to look at, like staring at the sun for too long.

"You've been following me? *Why?*" I demanded.

"Why, I've just told you. I wish to serve you. Believe me, I mean you no harm. Now please, no more questions until I eat. I'm hungry — *starving*. I haven't eaten for months...have some pity." He looked kind of pathetic, his warped face twisting into a bedraggled expression of longing.

My brow pinched as I tried to think of what to do. A sympathetic part of me really wanted to give him something, but I was afraid of what might happen if I did.

"This is a trap, isn't it? If I give you something, it's gonna come with some messed up consequences, won't it?" My voice still trembled, but I had started to regain my composure. Fascination was rapidly eclipsing my fright.

"No. In fact, if you get me some food, I'll give you something very special…something *wondrous*," the familiar hissed at me, his toothy jaws opening and making him look more cat-like.

A strange experience flooded my head as he whispered the words. I had a *vision* — and I don't mean that I saw anything with my eyes — but I could see it as clearly as if a film slide had folded over reality for a few seconds. I had *knowledge* of jewels hidden in the cavern all around me, glinting dully in the feeble light. They were unpolished, but thick and lustrous, and pulsed with their own luminesce. Yet as quickly as the echo of his words faded in my head, they too melted back into nothing.

"How do I know you're telling me the truth?" It was easily my biggest concern.

"Because familiars cannot lie. It's one of the inborn laws of our existence," he said, as if this should be quite obvious.

"There are others…like you? You have *laws*? Tell me them…." I coaxed, my fascination heightening.

"There are eleven others like me, so far as I know. As for laws…I cannot disobey a command from my master. I cannot tell anything that is not asked of me. I cannot take what is not given to me. I cannot enter where I am not invited…the list goes on. Now, please, I beg of you — mercy. Have mercy!" he yowled, pacing back and forth, so very catlike now.

"What exactly will you give me?" I prodded further, and he hissed at me, his fangs bared and his eyes blazing, sending a shock through my heart.

"*MERCY.*"

"All right, calm down!" I cried, fear rekindling in my chest. My shivering hands fumbled with the zipper on my bag and I fished frantically around inside until I found the granola bar I'd packed earlier that day for a snack. I tossed it to him gingerly, then my hands flew straight to my necklace and gripped. The familiar sniffed at the foil-wrapped treat for a moment, then looked back to me, the black slits that were his pupils fixed with unwavering precision.

"Not this. I need something else—something more *alive*," he moaned in a voice that was as demanding as it was tortured.

"I don't have anything else," I admitted.

"You've got hair. You've got skin. You've got nails... and lovely eyelashes, and *eyeballs*, and blood. Any of those things would be simply *scrumptious*..." he murmured, his long pink tongue licking at his jaws and his eyes narrowing to burning slits.

I worried I might vomit. "You wanna eat—no way! Get away from me! *Go on, leave me alone!*" I shrieked, wishing he would move so I could escape from this miserable cave without having to touch the demonic little beast.

Just as I thought it was going to turn into a struggle, he complied, slinking around me while tracking me with those bright eyes. He headed deeper into the cave, still watching me over his shoulder.

"All right, Sarah, I'll go, but you'd do well to remember how I'm suffering down here. Remember how I'm waiting down here for you. I'll settle for other things, you know. If you happen to have a change of mind or heart, just set a bowl of milk outside your window tonight; that will do. Give me some milk, and I'll bring you the thing you desire most in this world," he purred, the hideous grin still fixed on his face.

I squinted at him, halting my crawl out of that dismal cavern. "And what exactly is it that I want most?"

"To escape."

4

I HOISTED MYSELF up out of the cave and over the stone block, then set off at the fastest run I could muster. My legs didn't last long though, and I slid on the sandy pathway and lost my balance. Covered in clay and dirty water, shaking from head to foot, I felt like I was floating miles above my head. Whatever presence I had encountered down in those caves — familiar spirit, ghost, or figment of my imagination — the feeling of energy that surrounded it had dissipated. It was gone. I was safe for now, but I wasn't sure whether it would come back looking for food.

Blood.

I rose to my feet with a moan and scaled the hill. The meadow seemed miles wide, and I staggered over to the bus stop to await the next ride back to Merrill. I must've looked as shaken as I felt, because the bearded student next to me kept glancing over. He opened his mouth to ask what I assumed was going to be "Are you okay?" but when my wide, frantic eyes met his, he looked away. His reaction sobered me, and I was reminded of something that had occurred the week after

Lea died. My parents were both away that afternoon, and it was one of the hottest, stickiest days of summer. I had awakened late, around one, and right away the anguish had hit. The realization that Lea had been moving around, laughing, talking with me, lying on her bed and thinking — all just a week ago — and now was so abruptly and completely *gone* ruined any chance of a normal day.

I had plummeted into one of the most acute bouts of sorrow that I'd ever experienced and ended up collapsing on the couch. I'd gotten it together long enough to know that I needed help, and called who I'd thought of as my best friend at that point. Annie had been watching some show — *Supernatural*, I think — with our other friend, Jess, but when I called them, they drove right over. I don't know what I expected. They'd patted me on the back for a while, then just sat on the floor while I lay there, my eyes open and leaking tears. They stared, shaken by the intensity of my reaction.

"What do I *do*?" I had croaked. They looked at each other, at a loss for words.

"Stay busy, I guess. Just get your mind off things," Annie suggested without any conviction, as if she knew the best she could do wasn't very much at all. They were quiet for five minutes longer while I continued to cry, paralyzed and staring. Then one of them — I can't remember who — started talking about the episode they'd just been watching. An excited conversation followed, all while I was rendered defeated in the darkest hour of my life.

The memory of this kept me lucid on my way home. I couldn't process what I'd seen just yet, and I stood in front of the towering, crimson-leafed tree back at the Merrill dorms like a child who had lost sight of its mother. I didn't want to be alone right now, but the thought of talking to anyone made me sick.

I escaped into the community room and threw myself into a chair. Attached to the ceiling were these little rainbow twinkle lights that shifted colors to create the illusion they were moving in a line. I watched the other kids go about their business. Playing pool. Scrolling through blogs and other websites. Exchanging stories with their friends.

It all seemed so gut-wrenchingly meaningless, and it scared me that I thought so. What had I seen down in the caves? What had it done to me?

I remained motionless in that chair until dusk, feeling shell-shocked and disconnected. However, I couldn't ignore my rumbling stomach forever and ventured to the dining hall for something to eat, though I felt like I might retch it all back up afterward. As I stood in line and paid for my plate of mystery chicken and string beans, I thought about calling my mom and telling her what had happened. The idea was absurd.

Most of the friends I knew from Monterey didn't want to be associated with me now — I'd become too depressing after Lea died, and they complained I'd given up on life and resigned myself to being a downer until they couldn't deal with me anymore — so looking to one of them to talk to was out. I sat down and poked at the food on my plate, trying to come up with a "step one", and my eyes fell on the buffet line. There were cartons of milk stacked up there. Nonfat. One percent. Whole. A regular Smorgasbord of choices.

...but you'd do well to remember how I'm suffering down here.

And what if I *did* do it? What if I fed the little abomination? Would it cost me anything besides the perils of sneaking food out of the dining hall? If I set out some milk for him and he came back, at least I'd know that I was still sane, and that whatever was happening to me was beyond comprehension...or if he didn't show, I'd know that I was certifiable and I should seek anti-psychotics as soon as possible.

The thought of those ephemeral jewels glittering in the darkness beckoned to me, too. I wanted to see them again, or at least understand what they'd represented. That ghostly image was the only thing that haunted me as much as his revolting, hypnotizing eyes. I was tempted by the promise of something — what was the word the familiar had used — *wondrous?* It might be something earth-shaking, something that would allow me to escape the prison of malaise that my life had become. And it would only cost a carton of milk. If it's there, why not? *All right, Salem. You're getting the works. I won't skimp on your meal, pal, no sir-ee.* I abandoned my half-eaten meal and plucked a carton of whole milk off the counter, glancing back at the front of the dining hall. The rat-faced man who monitored dining students sort of had his eye on me. That creep never stopped smiling and that smile only seemed to get bigger when he caught someone trying to get past his guard with extra food stuffed under their coat. I waited till he started a random security check on a boy stoned out of his mind, then stuffed the milk carton into my bag. It stuck out at an odd angle next to my computer. This was going to be a bit of a challenge. I sauntered up to the gate, trying to appear as bored as possible. Smiley Guy must have smelled the delinquency on me, though, and raised his hand as I tried to leave.

"Hey, there — what's that in your bag? You got any food?" That smile never faltered. This guy was good.

I'd forgotten to come up with a just-in-case-I'm-caught lie, so I blurted out the only thing I could think of that would get him to leave me alone. "In my bag? Tampons. A lot of 'em."

Smiley Guy was a bit taken aback, and I felt a little surge of victory that I'd broken his grin, even if it was just for a second. He wasn't buying it, though.

"Let me see."

I pushed past him in a brusque motion and set off into a sprint, my tennis legs helping me get away. So I might get in trouble later. I didn't really care. I kept on running, feeling beautifully antisocial and freer than I had in weeks. The running started to feel less necessary and more instinctual after I was in the clear, and I broke into a wild gallop that carried me all the way back to my dorm room.

I DIDN'T HAVE a bowl, nor did I have tableware of any kind, so I dug a Styrofoam coffee cup out of the garbage, washed it out in the sink and set it on the windowsill. After night had fallen, I opened the window to the chill of the night and poured the milk into the cup. Then I sat back at my desk and waited for my good friend Thackery Binx to come crawling up to my window to get his long-awaited dinner.

He's been following me...he knows all about me, my name... what does he want? Thoughts darted in and out of my mind like frightened mice, but I kept my eyes fixed on that coffee cup, fully aware that I had to be stupid or insane to attempt this— or perhaps some brilliant combination of the two. I decided to Google *familiar spirits*, but what I read alarmed me, so I shut my computer, even less certain about what I was doing. After about an hour of tense waiting, my phone chimed with the sound of an incoming text from Joy:

```
Hey, Sarah. I just wanted to say how sorry
I am for earlier. I didn't mean to upset
you.
```

I cringed, remembering with the dead weight of shame how rude I'd been to Joy. I rubbed my forehead and scolded myself for the thousandth time, wishing it had been anyone but Joy that I'd exploded at. I fiddled with my necklace for a moment, then quickly answered:

```
No, I should be the one to apologize. I
acted like a bitch to you and you were
only trying to help. I didn't mean what I
said.
```

Dots appeared, telling me Joy had started to type something back, but I never got to see what it was. I glanced over at the window to double check on the cup, only to find it had disappeared. I rushed to the window and looked out into the bushes, my heart thundering.

Why did I do this? What possessed me? I asked myself, wondering if it was too late to take it back. The more I looked around outside, however, the calmer I grew. It was windy with a hint of rain in the air, but I could see nothing that hinted Sylvester had been the one to prowl up and take my offering.

I had just taken a few steps backward with the intent of shutting the window tight and hiding in my bed for the rest of the evening when a pair of ghostly green eyes blinked at me from the crimson tree outside. Its bright leaves, still vibrant in the night, shook and whipped about in the gales, but he stayed perched there, still and licking his lips. Our eyes connected for a long while, the wind whistling around and rainy mist splattering my face.

"Come with me," I heard him call me from far away, though his voice sounded as close as if he'd whispered in my ear. Without waiting for my response, he leapt from the lofty branches and floated down to the ground in slow motion. He landed without a sound on the damp soil, then streaked off into the angry redwoods.

I was too scared to move at first, and at the first flash of lightning I was almost certain that nothing in this world could have called me out into that violent night. But just as the first patters of rain rolled over the sill and onto the threadbare carpet with its years of dirt beaten into it by the feet of so many strangers, I decided that I needed to go. I had already pushed past something that I could never undo. If I stayed where I was, I'd be forever half-formed. I knew too much to live peacefully ever again; the memory of this day and all its eerie possibilities would nag me into madness if I let it slip away. The gates had been closed behind me and there was no way out but forward, so forward I went.

I pulled on my hooded, knit poncho in a flurry and hurried out into the night. The direction the creature had gone in wasn't clear, so I kept following a path that just felt right and ended up at a pair of electrical towers that looked like the silhouettes of skeletons against the clouded sky of opaline gray. When the lightning flashed again, I saw him atop the fence around the towers. My heart fluttered in that awful, painful concoction of excitement and fright.

"Where are we going?" I shouted over the wind to him, but he just kept on smiling and leapt down. I ran after that bushy tail as it snaked through the underbrush, my boots getting muddier by the moment. Soon I lost track of where I was and where I was headed. I became a greyhound after the rabbit, something ancient igniting inside of my brain. Is there anything more primal than a chase?

I came out of my frenzied run once I had burst into a dark clearing with a bed of overgrown ferns and dried up pine leaves. The rain was making a soup of this, and a frothy, muddy foam was starting to swirl about. In the center of that mess was little Figaro, ever the patient guide.

"Come closer, Sarah. Look what I've made for you," he coaxed me, sounding almost giddy. His whiskers prickled as I inched closer to where he sat on his haunches with something on the ground between his paws. Still full of dread that he might attack at any moment, I approached and saw a little golden box with a bronze-colored taffeta bow atop the lid. It looked like a little birthday present.

"What is it?" I breathed, and he looked down at it for a moment, then back up at me.

"What does it look like?"

"Like a box."

"Then that's what it is. Open it up. Find out what's inside!" he squealed with delight, a feline sound that matched the pitch of the wind singing through the pines.

My numb fingers reached forward and lifted the box, no longer than an inch and a half. I opened it and became certain that this was all a dream. I wondered, in a moment of sublime madness, if I was in a coma like Stephen, or trapped in a long, vivid nightmare. Inside the box was a perfectly preserved bit of my past—a petit four cake. When Lea and I were little, the bank our dad worked at was next to a bakery. When Mom called and told him we'd been good that day, he'd come home with petit fours, one for everyone in the family. When he got a job elsewhere, those delightful little confections disappeared from our lives. Yet here one was. Baked in the exact style that store had made them in. The same iced roses, the same shape. There was no mistaking it.

"Where did you get this?" I gasped, shielding the sweet from the rain with the lid.

"I told you, I made it for you. In return for your generosity. Go on. Eat it up. I know you'll find it to your liking," Jiji purred.

"It's poison, isn't it?" My head was starting to reel. The petit four was giving off a strong, sugary scent that made my mouth water and lust after its taste. I somehow knew its flavor would perfectly match my memories. The more I breathed in its aroma, the dizzier I felt.

"What do you mean by 'poison?'" he questioned, confused.

"It'll make me sick. It'll kill me," I heard my own voice say. I was frightened most because I was having such a hard time resisting. I wanted that little rose on top, the silky green frosting, the creamy marzipan inside, the fluffy layers of cake....

"It's not that kind of poison. It will just help you escape. It won't hurt you. Try some and see...."

5

WHAT DID IT matter if it was poison, even the kind that would kill me? Felix the cat — *the wonderful, wonderful cat* — had known that what I craved most was escape, and in those few moments I realized that he was absolutely correct. I wanted to break free of my life as it was.

As this aching longing came over me, I lost control. In a frantic motion, I plucked the cake out of the box and shoved it into my mouth, feverishly chewing as the explosion of flavor swept over my tongue. It was worlds better than I remembered, so enticingly delectable that my heart and head fluttered. The light sweetness and soft cream blended together to form an experience I imagined heaven would be like. I wanted it to last forever, but I was so hungry for its taste that I gobbled it down in seconds. After I swallowed, I began to pant. Panic set in. I'd actually done it. There was no going back. Now I'd just have to wait and see what escape really meant.

"Am I gonna be okay?" I wailed, the words spouting from my lips like steam from a kettle. My legs felt weak and I didn't know whether it was from nerves or if the petit four had reached its destination.

"You're going to be more than okay. Just let it slide over you…I'll guide you all the way there…." Salem's voice soothed, comforting now, evoking memories of youth and safety. I grew even more afraid.

What have I done? What have I done? I've got to stop this, somehow.

Drowsiness overwhelmed me and I sank to the ground. The bed of wet needles now seemed like a bed of feathers and silks. I lay my head down as Binx circled me, a shark around a helpless rowboat. He was purring, and the noise lulled me even further toward sleep. The rain sounded softer now and far away, and as my lids grew heavier and blinking them turned laborious, I marveled at how gorgeous the boughs of the trees looked when crystallized by the downpour. If this was dying, then dying was beautiful.

Felix's circling was hypnotic, and my eyes attempted to track him with each ring he made around my body, which had drawn into the fetal position of its own accord.

What came next is still too foggy for me to remember. It was that sacred zone between waking and sleep, where your mind is just barely clinging on to the things that make sense in the world but looking forward with rapture toward the infinite possibility of dreams and the fathomless peace that lies in the darkness on the other side of them. Years could've gone by. I didn't care. I was in heaven, floating on my little cloud of needles and leaves.

The thing that drew me from my stupor were his green, green eyes. They were above me now, bobbing. The more I focused on them, the higher they got. They beckoned for me to follow, and I did. We rose a few inches, then a few feet into the air, my head feeling like it was filling with helium. I made the mistake of looking down.

I was above my body. I saw it lying there in the mud and rainwater, my chest still rising and falling gently. I tried to scream and it came out as a wave of dark ripples of bent light around me. I was stuck. I couldn't budge from where I was, and at that point in my life I had never experienced a terror so complete. It felt like hours, hovering there and watching myself sleep, but then I saw his eyes again. They swam into my vision, and that comforting feeling of home quieted my tempestuous heart.

Follow me, the eyes seemed to say, and I found that I could move freely once again. We were swimming now, upward into the air and gaining speed by the second. We pierced through the weepy cloud cover and its halo of mist, then through the atmosphere. I was too stunned by the beauty of the stars to feel afraid now, and as I let those brilliant, cold points of light fill my vision they began to expand. The light was growing, blinding me, but it didn't hurt at all; it was peaceful. It surrounded me, and I was traveling through it.

I have no memory of the time between then and when I returned to consciousness. My eyes focused and I sat up slowly, a shower of shining sand falling from my hair and shoulders.

I was on a beach with silvery sand. The fragments were fine and sparkled in the rosy light of a velvety, vibrant sunset that looked too beautiful to be real.

The first eccentricity that struck me was that while I was on a beach, I felt none of the unpleasant things about being at the beach—no chill in the wind, no smells of sunbaked kelp, no gnats buzzing around, no sand that crept into my shoes, no sticks or rocks in the surf. The air was sharp and my unfamiliar surroundings uncomfortably clear. The only way I can describe it is that my senses *stretched*. Sight, smell, touch…everything went farther. I was aware of it, but didn't feel threatened. Every-thing was hyper-pleasurable. As this sensation intensified, I saw in the distance a pier with an amusement park perched on it, everything spinning and trickling with rainbows, flooding me with its motion and the sounds of merriment.

"You made it," a voice purred from behind and I swiveled around to see a placid Felix standing in the sand.

"What did you do to me?" I breathed, more mystified than angry. "Am I dead? Is this heaven?"

"You're not dead. You're only sleeping. Well, your body is, back where you left it," he explained and my brow furrowed.

"But then…what is all *this*?" I pointed to myself. I looked corporeal. I *felt* corporeal.

"Your body is the vehicle for your consciousness. That's what you are now. Consciousness freed from a material prison. Everything you see before you is a product of thought. You are in complete control of this portion of this world. This place is what I call my garden. Except now it belongs to you, Sarah."

"What? Why? And why does it look this way if I didn't make it that way?" I demanded, stumbling up to the surf and running my fingers through the waves. It was as warm as bathwater.

"It remained in the condition it was left in by the last person who owned it," he answered, prancing up to where I stood. There were tiny, bright colored fish swimming in the shallows and he batted at them lazily. "And it's yours because you fed me. It's the reward I promised."

I shuddered from a sudden rush of lightness, as if a great weight had been ripped off my shoulders. It was too good to be true, yet here I was, standing in the middle of it. Proof before my very eyes. Even if this wasn't really happening, I was perceiving it just as clearly, or perhaps even *more* clearly, than the real world.

A dark thought halted my reverie. "Wait, will I be here forever?" I worried aloud, and the familiar shook his head.

"This will fade, which is why it is my strong suggestion you start to take advantage of your time here sooner rather than later," he told me with apparent boredom, then made a small noise of victory as he caught a neon orange fish in his claws and gobbled it down.

"I thought you weren't allowed to take anything without asking?" I asked, and his stomach-churning grin widened.

"I told you, nothing here is real, but it will all *feel* real. Go on. Try it. Make something," he encouraged and I frowned.

He could tell I hadn't the slightest idea how to do what he'd suggested. He sighed, took up a mouthful of sand, and then leapt into the air. He floated up as if riding the breeze and whirled around to drop the sparkling grains onto my outstretched palm. "Will it, and it shall be."

"Okay," I said, concentrating on the sand. *I want...more petit fours.*

The sand quivered and glowed, then shifted into a cyclone of light that reformed as a silver plate laden with the pastel-colored snacks. I laughed with delight, plucked one off the plate and popped it into my mouth. A symphony of flavor sang on my taste buds, unlike anything I'd ever tasted before. Even the unearthly cake that had brought me here paled in comparison. After I'd had a moment to revel in the joy of such a creation, I finished off the plate with the vigorous appetite of a puppy faced with a full bowl of food.

"And I don't even feel full!" I exclaimed as I set the ornate silver plate down in the sand. "This is fantastic! This is incredible!" My head was buzzing, the overwhelming possibilities reducing me to a temporary state of shock.

"I told you you'd like it. Now, make more food! Make a whole *feast*." The spirit bounced on his paws, leaping up high into the air and floating down gracefully, as if he were sinking through water and not air.

"That is an excellent idea, um—what do I call you? What's your name?" I faltered, wondering why I'd never bother to ask the creature before this moment.

He stopped bouncing. "I have no name, or at least not one that I can tell you. You must give me one. I'm yours now, after all."

My joy wavered. Something about the idea of *owning* this little demon brought on feelings of trepidation.

"A name? I don't know. I'll just call you...Felix. For now, I guess. Until I think of something better," I said and shrugged, turning back to infinity with avarice. I lifted my hands up like a conductor at his podium, and out of the sand formed a table covered with a silk, embroidered cloth. With more flicks of my fingers, dishes divine and sumptuous materialized out of the gold dust. Apples, grapes, pears, nectarines, peaches, berries—all saturated with sun-given sweetness, luscious and almost bursting with juices—sprang into existence aside braised meats caramelized with glazes of sauce. Massive, moist turkeys surrounded with ruby-bright cranberries, troughs of potatoes, steamy with a light, garlic scent, and ribs dripping with thick sauce followed. There were hot rolls, crumbly cornbread, and soups fit for a king. Icy pitchers of juice, honeyed wines, and jugs of crisp, refreshing water joined the procession. More and more the feast built itself with every food I loved, and when I willed confections that I had never imagined or heard of, they too joined the culinary parade. This pleased me most of all—this strange world wasn't limited by my own imagination.

I could hold back no longer. Felix and I attacked the table and every last one of the victuals, forsaking any form of manners in our frenzied hunger. We ate like hyenas upon a fresh kill, and not even for an instant did a feeling of sickness or tightness of the belly come upon me. When I had finished with the feast, I threw myself down into the sand, laughing in disbelief and contentment, with the satisfying sensation that I'd finished a moderately sized meal. Just as I grew sleepy while enjoying the tapestry of dusty colors that was the eternal sunset, Felix's bright eyes came into my vision.

"What are you waiting for? There's so much more you can do. Think, Sarah. Dream. Bring it all into creation," Felix coaxed, and I sat back up. I hesitated, then decided to forge ahead. If the clock really was ticking....

I took off at a run toward the pier with the wild amusement park twirling and blinking atop its platform. I gathered speed and right as I reached the point on the sand where the waves were crashing, I took a little hop, then a leap, and I was gliding through the air. I skimmed above the waves, my heart skipping beats and a laugh ricocheting around in my throat. Felix was beside me now, and we both gained altitude, sailing next to that brilliant disc of light that was the sun, landing atop the Ferris wheel.

We rode it, marveling at all the attractions below us and the small crowd enjoying them. I understood that none of the people around us were real; not the beaming children tugging at the hands of their parents, nor the young lovers cooing to each other in the other gondolas. They were all part of the illusion of the garden; puppet shows created to stave off loneliness. We floated from each ride and carnival booth to the next: the unrestrained speed of the roller coaster, the mystery of the fortune telling tent, the shocks of the ghost house. My senses were overloaded with bobbing balloons, the smells of caramel popcorn mixed with cotton candy, and fireworks exploding above us. When we had exhausted what was there, I raised up the ocean level and flooded the park, submerging the glimmering rainbow of lights. We rose with the water level, watching the fair below us, still operational within the sea. I took one last look at it, warmth filling my heart, and then wiped it clean.

My desires unfolded one by one. My own island, complete with a three-story tree house. A million dollar shopping-spree in New York City. A stroll through an enchanted botanical dreamscape where Felix and I chased after pixies and sprites.

I had always wanted to slay a dragon, too, so I brought that to reality. I couldn't ever remember feeling so powerful and in control as when I lopped off the beast's head while its blood dripped down my sword, drops of scarlet molasses. I decided next to go to a fancy ball where I chatted idly with Shakespeare, Abraham Lincoln, and Stanley Kubrick, and right in the middle of the affair the whole soiree came to a hush and I was presented an award for being a visionary photographer. As I was taking my bows and being lauded by too many famous faces to count, Felix nodded to me. We waved goodbye, then split through the ceiling, only to go sailing in a skiff across the Milky Way. Celestial insects all aglow with their own luminescence fluttered by: butterflies, ladybugs, fireflies, jeweled beetles with opal wings.

"Felix, this is…this is the most wonderful thing in the universe. I don't ever want to leave," I told him, the sleeves of my gossamer gown flowing in the breeze as I dragged my hand through the starry stream. It was pleasantly cool. Felix crept over and curled up in my lap.

How was I ever afraid of you? I thought with something very much like affection in my heart, stroking his fur and scratching behind his ears. We floated there for a while, drifting blissfully on the sea of stars until I wiped it clean and created an autumn forest set aflame with the light of a sunset, the air crisp with a hint of cinnamon and smoke floating on the breeze. I asked the animals to come out and spend some time with us, and became so immersed in the grand time we were having waltzing and singing in the forest hollow I didn't notice a strange sensation creeping up on me at first, invading my joyful world.

It was another person. I could feel them, unlike the projections of my imagination or the dancing animals and children amusement park. It was another soul.

"Felix, what's happening? Can you—can you feel that?" I looked down in concern at the familiar, his nod reassuring me.

"You needn't worry. It's only someone coming into your garden for a visit. One of the others. Someone's curious to see this garden occupied after being empty so long." Felix turned toward the leaf-covered slope, blazing with the burnt orange and cranberry reds of the foliage.

I watched with him, until movement disturbed the hill above and a face came into view. A pair of round, honey-colored eyes blinked back at me as a boy, maybe one or two years my senior, stepped up to the crest of the hill with feet well-practiced in hiking. The bones in his bewildered face were well-defined, his dark brown hair messy. He wore a well-loved wool sweater and scratchy brown trousers. Thirty seconds passed in silence before I spoke.

"Hello," I said, lifting my hand in salutation. He turned and ran, kicking up a shower of autumn leaves behind him.

"Wait! What's wrong?" I yelled, trying to use my new sense of control over this world to shrink its vastness, but he'd pierced through what I sensed to be the boundaries of my garden and was gone. Confused, I bid the dancing animals—they had been consumed with festivities during the encounter—to run off into the woods and leave Felix and me. I turned down to the familiar and asked, "Who was that?"

"I think his name is Angus. He calls his familiar Aodh. I rather like that spirit, too. He's one of the others that makes eternity bearable," Felix said, making my brain flood with the curiosities surrounding him.

"You said there are eleven other spirits, right? And each of them has a human partner?" I asked, and Felix nodded, patient and attentive. "So where did you come from? Where did this place come from?"

"I don't know. I don't remember that far back. It's always been here, and so have we. I can't remember being born any more than you can. I've been going to your world since the dark times, the times of fire, the times of ice. We all did. We've all had many names, and many faces. The times without creatures that can use words are terrible ones, full of chaos—we sit those times out and wait. Wait for refined consciousness to return to the physical world," Felix murmured, hypnotizing my mind into visions of primordial Earth. The sun began to sink in the distance and the forest around us grew darker. The breeze kicked up and a chill I hadn't willed there ran through it.

"And you don't want to hurt the people who feed you, do you?"

"No, we don't want to hurt you. We *love* you. You sustain us. You entertain us. You maintain us," he chanted, his eyes glowing too bright.

"And the others—can I speak to them? Can I go to their gardens the way that boy came into mine?"

Felix nodded. "Of course. But you won't be in control there. You've got to be careful with a few of them. Not everyone is receptive to visitors in their private world. The little one and the old woman would probably like to meet you. Stella speaks your language, and she's here right now. I can take you to them, if you like," Felix offered, his tail twitching.

After a moment of deliberation I nodded. I wanted to talk to another person, someone who knew what was going on and could give me an explanation I could trust. Felix was…*fantastical*, but I still didn't know if I could believe his words.

6

THE FAMILIAR LED me through the woods of my own creation, and when we reached the edge of the world that I had inherited—*or taken?*—we stepped through something like a thin membrane of palpable, invisible energy. My skin tingled as I looked around, finding that we now stood in a beautiful little meadow. It looked like something out of a fairy tale; a cottage as precious and overly florid as the ones Thomas Kinkade painted was nestled in the grass, complete with a waterwheel spinning over a stream. Behind the cozy home was a forest, the floor carpeted with flowers of many colors.

Before I could step through the knee-high grass, I heard a little cry from behind the home, and then a little girl was running toward me at full speed, her arms outstretched and a beaming smile on her lips. She was as pretty as a picture, and looked just like a porcelain doll with her rosy cheeks and blonde curls. Tiny arms curled around my leg as the child sang out in French.

Above her fluttered a massive butterfly with oddly shaped wings, whose entire form hummed with wisdom and power. Every time it flapped its wings, they seemed to shine in a different iridescent hue and if I looked at it too long, I felt dreamy, like I was slipping away from this world. I sensed it knew me—knew what I was thinking, and could speak to me if it liked, yet remained silent as I stared at those mesmerizing wings with their changing patterns and colors. I shook my head. These two were as real as the boy in my garden had been. I could feel the girl's soul brimming with love for me, though I hardly knew why.

"*Blanche!*" called a female voice from inside the cottage. This French sounded different than the little girl's, as if the speaker had a strong accent. "*Reviens vite, toute suite! Pischouette, c'est dangereux à l'extérieur, maintenant! Qui est...*" The huffy woman stepped outside, her words trailing off as she noticed me. Her black eyes searched me the way the boy's had, but instead of running, her face broke into a welcoming smile, stained with a deep sadness I could not understand.

"*Ma, jamais d'la vie...elle est la defante.* Hey, girl, what they call you?" she pointed to me as she spoke, the child still chattering away in French.

It took me a moment to piece together what she had asked. It had sounded like '*Ey, gaal. Wut dey caah ya*'. "Er, Sarah. I'm Sarah."

The old woman nodded and shut her eyes, then beckoned me to come closer. I complied, the little girl romping alongside me. The old woman had big, round eyes with yellowish whites. The skin of her face was soft, papery, and showered signs of age, but wasn't very wrinkled. A scarf wrapped around her head tinkled with little beads and crystals, and many different shawls of varying shades of purple were wrapped about her shoulders.

I couldn't contain my questions. "Please, ma'am—can you tell me...well, anything about this place? I'm—I'm kinda lost, I guess you could say, I—"

"Hush now, child. Come on inside. I'll tell you 'bout everything. This here est ma petite Blanche's Garden. I'm a visitor here too, but she seem to like you fine," the old woman laughed, her voice hoarse but amiable. I couldn't imagine there being any danger here, so I followed her into the cottage, the little girl still hopping at my heels.

The inside was just as lovely as the exterior. Porcelain cups, rustic furniture, home-sewn quilts, and vases bursting with flowers picked from the meadow were crammed inside the cozy space. It looked like a replica of Snow White's cottage, complete with the pies sitting on the windowsills. We sat at a worn, wooden table with gentle light streaming in through the stained glass and coloring the room. The butterfly landed on the chair where the little girl sat, its wings still dreamily flapping even though it was not airborne. I couldn't keep my eyes off the wings, no matter how I tried, and my head ached in the same way Felix's eyes caused it to. The old woman bustled about, making tea for the three of us as she spoke kindly to the little girl in French, as if explaining something that a child her age would not easily comprehend. When she was done and three steaming mugs of tea that smelled strongly of herbs sat before us, she turned to me with her dark, hazy eyes and gave me her full attention.

"First you tell Mama Stella, child, how it is you come here." Beneath her thick Cajun accent her voice was motherly, though it didn't quite make me feel safe. There was something powerful behind that kindly gaze that I didn't feel like testing, so I stuck to the truth.

"I—I gave some food to him," I pointed at Felix, who had followed us into the kitchen, "and he offered me a cake, and I ate it and—"

"And it take you here. To the Unreal City," Mama Stella finished with an understanding smile.

"Unreal City? Is that what this place is? Is that how you all get here? Please, tell me more," I begged. I just knew my time here wouldn't last for very much longer — I could feel the heightened sense of reality already fading, especially when I looked at that butterfly. I wanted to know exactly what I was getting into, and what it might cost me if I ever wanted to come back.

"It what the man in the library call it, so most of us Cunning Folk come to call it that too, but it never had no true name," she explained. "And what bring us here is something different for each one — a tiny bottle of sweet liquor for me, a *bon bon* for *cher* Blanche, so she tells me. It's our heads that make it look different, make it look *tempting*. But my podna Mardi tell me it all the same stuff — only they the ones can make it."

"Podna Mardi?"

"Ah weh, girl, my friend the spirit. Come on in here, Mardi," she called into the back room of the cottage, and the sound of hooves on wood approached. An animal that at first looked to be an oversized ram with golden wool clopped around the doorway, and I shuddered at the sight of its face. Instead of the sheep's head that should've been at the end of its fleecy neck, there was a solid gold carnival mask. Elaborate horns sprouted on either side; emeralds, amethysts, and a plume of feathers decorating them. I couldn't see any eyes behind that mask, but the jewels glimmered with that ethereal light that made my head fuzzy. It was looking straight at me, feeling what I felt and pillaging my memories.

"Please, tell me everything you know. I don't think I have much time left," I insisted, willing myself to look away from the familiar.

"There sure ain't time for that, but here's the basics. Your spirit cannot lie to you, and he *must* do what you say once you enter a pact with him, but he always try to trick you, too. Just you gotta ask him the right questions, weh?" Mama Stella said, a twinkle in her eye. "You be careful 'bout what you give him too, be careful 'bout how many times you come here unless you sure you want it always—things start to seem different, back home, too. Don't be scared of what you see. They can't hurt you none. But stay in the right places here, 'cause there's things here that can. Don't never go looking for trouble, peesh-wank, don't go digging deep in the Unreal City. Stay where your friends stay. That's why I stay here with her, ma Blanche. She can't wake up, anymore—she say there was a car accident in her life, and now she's sleeping forever. I just make sure her dreams is always nice."

The old woman looked upon the little girl, who was sip-ping at the steaming cup and licking her lips. My heart ached for her. She might forever be frozen at this age, in a state of unchanging innocence, until she died. I knew that if I ever came back to this place—to Unreal City—then I would want to spend some time with her.

"Now come here, Sarah. I know what is your kind of girl— you not gonna heed my warning," Mama Stella said, standing up and gesturing for me to do the same. "So I'm gonna help you out, silly as you is."

I rose alongside my anger, opening my mouth to protest her criticism, but the old woman hushed me with her raised finger. The ram moved its head back and forth, the beads, coins, and jewels adorning its body tinkling. Mama Stella studied me, then shut her eyes and took a deep breath in through her nose.

"Hang on, a minute, what are you going to do to me?!" I cried.

Before I could stop her, the old woman lifted two fingers and touched them to my pendant. The brief contact sent an electric current flowing through the chain of the necklace and buzzing down to my chest, making me gasp and double over. I caught my breath and looked up at her, shocked tears in my eyes.

"What the hell was that? What did you do?"

"I gave you a charm for protection. I want no harm to come to you child, that's why I done it." Mama Stella's dark eyes were passionate, but I was already withdrawing, my hands clasped over my pendant.

How dare she touch this...does she know?

"Thanks for your help, but I've got to be going," I barked, making for the door.

Little Blanche leapt from her seat, looking back and forth from me to Mama Stella in confusion. Mama Stella nodded, that sadness overtaking her again, and waved her hands in the direction of the door.

"Please take care out there, child. You come back here too. You always welcome. Come back," she pleaded as I made my retreat, Felix scampering after me.

My breathing was agitated and my heart pounded as we made for the edge of Blanche's Garden. "Felix, what did she do to me?" I panted as I walked, not daring to look back.

"What she said she did," he replied, calm and confusing as always.

I wasn't sure I was in the mood to dissect potential meaning behind this, so I charged onward until I stepped through the thin layer of cellophane-like energy separating the gardens. I thought I'd been going back to mine, but found I had stumbled into another stranger's world. Things were starting to look less focused now, but I could tell I was on a beach at night, though it was neither tropical nor rocky like the ones in California. It was nestled between green mountains, and the sand was soft beneath my toes.

In the sky was a dazzling display of aurora borealis. A few feet away stood a little hut with a thatched roof and paper screens. I took a moment to study this, then noticed a slender, middle-aged woman approaching in the dim lavender light. She seemed glad to see me, her smile reaching her eyes. She took my hand in hers, holding it for a moment before letting go.

"Hello," I said, comforted by her presence, the threat of the electric shock already fading from my nerves.

"*Youkoso,*" was her reply. The tone of her voice was soothing, but I shook my head to show I didn't understand her. "*Hajimemashite, atashi ha Masami...namae ha Masami. Masami desu. Kore ha Masami no niwa yo.*" She pointed to her chest, repeating *Masami* until I guessed that she must be telling me her name.

"Oh, um, Sarah. I'm Sarah," I said and pointed to myself.

She nodded and gestured for me to come to the shore, and we sat down together in the sparkling sands to watch the aurora. I tried to communicate details about who I was, and she did the same. She kept making little motions as if she were casting a line, and I guessed her daily life had something to do with fishing. We gave up and just enjoyed the lights in the sky.

A pair of iridescent jellyfish floated by in mid-air, glowing as if under a black light and connected by their tentacles. Masami laughed, a pleasant sound, and Felix leapt up to join them. They spun around together in the sky, silent communication ensuing as the jellyfish pulsated with that particular type of light that seemed to be the familiar spirits' energy.

"*Izanami...to Izanagi,*" Masami pointed to each of the jellyfish, then laughed as if she'd made a little joke. I laughed too to show I was listening, but the spirits' dance was making my head drift further and further away. My vision blurred until it was just a smudge of glittering lights on the black ocean waves, the shimmering waves of the aurora, and the floating tentacles in their pale luminescence. I stayed there until shadows washed in and wiped the color and light away, and a heavy sleepiness weighed down on my shoulders. I fell from Unreal City peacefully, with quiet in my heart and the gentle crashing of the waves in my ears.

7

WAKING UP WAS pure agony. I groaned into life, my joints aching, my throat and nose burning with sickness. My head was pounding like a jackhammer was going off inside it, and I was soaked through to the bone. A thick layer of mud and pine needles had ruined my clothing, and as I rose from the forest floor dripping, coughing, and sniffling, I wanted nothing more than to return to that place where no pain was allowed. I felt hundreds of pounds heavier as I rose to my feet and did the best to remove all the debris from my hair.

"How are you feeling, Sarah?" asked a voice, and I looked over my shoulder in surprise. He was still there. Felix had followed me home.

"I need to get home. I think I'm sick," I sniffed, and took a few steps in the direction I thought would lead me back.

Felix corrected me, and I followed him through the glistening ferns. The forest always seemed to shine too brightly the morning after the rain. I couldn't quite see things properly — my whole mode of perception seemed skewed. Every time I stopped to take a short break I would lean against a redwood tree and the entire tower of it felt alive. I was more aware than usual of its growth, of all the creatures that made its body their home, of the moss and lichens feeding off it. It was too overwhelming. I found it hard to care when my horrified hall mates saw me stumble in and make straight for the shower.

I spent the entire day in bed, staring at the ceiling and trying to make sense of all the things that had happened to me. Felix watched me from the corner, never making a peep but lashing his tail back and forth the whole time. I had questions aplenty for him, but I couldn't seem to bring myself to ask him and break the silence. Silence was what I needed, to try and organize the anarchy that had been set loose inside my brain.

I had to start from square one now. I had to rewrite everything I knew about life. It wasn't just whether Unreal City existed or not, it was that reality as I knew it had been altered forever. The worst part was, I would never have any true way of defining it. I knew things and had seen things that the scientific tools of today could never measure, that no one would ever be able to explain to me, or give proper names to. It was daunting, and I wondered if that was how our ancient ancestors had felt, staring up at the sky and catching a glimpse of lightning as it ignited the earth and split the sky. There was an extraordinary power in what I had been playing with; it something I could explore and use, but never, *ever* understand. Every time I looked around my room, I saw the objects that had only yesterday meant so much to me—felt so solid, so material—now they seemed like toy pieces in a board game. It felt like years had gone by since last night.

After spending hours in quiet contemplation, I rose to find a meal. I was hollow, and though I didn't know how I could keep any food down, I knew I had to try. Felix wanted to follow me, but something in his prowling form and ever-watchful eyes disturbed me, so I bid him to stay in my room and headed to the dining hall for dinner. The entire way there, I felt like I was walking underwater, as if the entire campus had become an aquarium.

The food was tasteless in my mouth, but it sustained me, and I decided to keep walking around after I finished my meal. Luckily, Smiley Guy didn't recognize me as the infamous milk thief and I escaped the cafeteria without incident. The trees with their red crowns of leaves shuddered as I walked by. I made my way up and down the campus until my feet were sore and my bones ached.

I returned that evening to my room and found Felix in the exact spot I'd left him. His bat ears quivered with excitement. "Did you bring me anything, Sarah?" he asked and I hesitated before shaking my head. Poisonous anger filled his eyes and he drew back his lips in a snarl.

Shocked, I held up my hands and attempted to placate him. "Tomorrow. I'll bring you something tomorrow," I promised, but he growled and began pacing the ground near my computer. My stomach started to twinge and I wondered if I was going to throw up after all.

"Felix, I have — I'm curious about certain things."

"Ask me."

I could tell his usual patience was wearing thin. "Can I go back again...to Unreal City?"

No matter what, his answer would be awful. If no, I would live the rest of my life empty, longing for the sweetness of that other world I was no longer allowed into. And if it were yes, it would alter my life, forever. I might even abandon it altogether, in search of greener pastures.

"If you feed me, I might let you go back again. And if you give me something a bit more satisfying, you'll be able to go back whenever you like until the day you die," Felix told me, that unsettling growl still in his throat.

"What are you talking about?"

"I mean right now if you decide to send me away or don't give me the nutrition I deserve, I'll disappear and search for another person to join the Cunning Folk. But if you offer me, say, your hair for example, I shall make my services available to you." Felix leapt up on the bottom bunk — *Lea's bed* — and I frowned at him.

I was starting to see what Mama Stella had meant. Felix never seemed to lie, but I couldn't quite get a straight answer out of him, either. "So if I bring you milk for a while, will you stay?"

"Yes."

"And will you let me go back?" I sounded desperate even to my own ears, and when he shook his head my heart leapt into my throat. "Why not?"

"I told you, I want something more. Give me your hair. You're not using it," Felix coaxed, and I touched my wispy blonde hair, considering. The idea unsettled me. I was sure there was another important detail he wasn't revealing. I had to be more precise in my questioning.

"Will there be any consequences if you eat it? For me, I mean? Will it change anything?"

Felix shook his head. "No, nothing will change. So will you do it?" His voice was high-pitched, excited and hopeful.

I faltered, sinking down into the desk chair as I thought. The things I'd witnessed there — the intrigue, the beauty — I needed it again. I needed the auroras and the romps through the forest and the star-sailing and the feeling of being in complete control. After tasting that once, I couldn't even consider going back to this life. All I had to look forward to here was a struggle through a mire of grief —

A horrible thought occurred to me. *If I can make anything happen in my garden....*

"I'll do it, but not until this weekend. You get milk until then, because I've got to go to school. But next Saturday you can have my hair. But you've got to take me there again. Is it a deal?" I offered him my hand, and he placed his paw on top of it, victory glittering in his smile.

THE FIRST THING I did after Sociology ended on Monday night was hurry over to Joy as she was standing up. She saw me coming and concern flashed across her face, though she offered an amiable wave.

"Joy," I stuttered, at a complete loss of how to relate to her how sorry I was. "I—look, I—"

"It's okay, Sarah. You don't have to say anything. I understand, it's..." she left off, and I felt a little relief flow through me. The old me begged to tell her I didn't know what she was talking about, that I had just came over to talk about the project, but my anger didn't seem to burn as glaringly this evening.

"Thanks, Joy. For understanding. Want to, um, like, get coffee and talk about the presence of scare tactics in the media, or something?" I offered. I repressed the urge to slap myself in the face. Where had this person come from? Sarah Wilkes had never stumbled over her words before college.

Joy flashed that signature heart-warming smile. "Yeah, that sounds good. When?"

"How about right now? At Cowell?" I asked, and felt another wave of relief when she seemed happy about the idea.

We left class together, walking side-by-side with our breath streaming out in clouds. I noticed a sticker of a mermaid on her phone, and made an errant comment about the "darling mermaid darlings" which set us off on a conversation about the quote's television origin. After discovering we were both big fans of *Pushing Daisies*, we chattered away about other shared interests as the temperature continued to drop.

By the time we'd pushed open the door to the coffee shop and made our order — we'd both decided to get a slice of pie in honor of Lee Pace's character's profession — we'd covered Neil Gaiman's novels, *Les Misérables*, Keanu Reeves, and how much we both adored cats. I got so wrapped up in debating the little things I cared about, I almost forgot that detached feeling that had consumed me since I'd returned from Unreal City. It seemed little more than a vivid dream as we unpacked our laptops and forced ourselves to work on our research paper.

"I'm still not sure where we should go with this, but I thought maybe we could look into news reports of crimes and how they are portrayed. I wonder if we can find any articles that would show just how much grisly details are exploited to scare the people who read or watch the news," Joy began, putting on her reading glasses and hitting keys with fervor. "You know, how sometimes they blow things out of proportion and make it seem like everyone is constantly in danger — things like supposed terrorist threats, sickness outbreaks, or over-the-top storm warnings. It's almost as if creating a general feeling of anxiety to promote their ratings and get viewers to tune in is more important than giving accurate information. They make everything into a 'feature' — just look at the graphics on the news and the catchy titles they create. Like it's a movie or something."

"That's a good starting point," I agreed, and began a few searches of my own on the topic.

We settled into working for about twenty minutes, scrawling things in notebooks. I'll be honest: I wasn't trying too hard. My thoughts weren't truly dedicated to work. The importance of school seemed to slip after what I'd seen and done, and without conversation my mind was drifting back to the delights I'd found on the astral plane. My heart leapt every time I considered what I was planning to do when I went there again. As I wondered for the thousandth time if I had the courage to attempt the most tempting of them all, Joy's voice disturbed my thoughts.

"Oh God, just listen to this: 'More Details Uncovered in Oregon Mass-Slaying: Twin Rivers, Oregon. Police have uncovered more about the shocking mass-murder that occurred sometime last Friday evening. Among the nine missing people, two performers, Samuel Baker, thirty-six, and Oliver Stout, forty, were found brutally mutilated in a local community theater, with a third member of their troupe, Simon Shaw, twenty-four, still missing. Police have identified a third burnt corpse, found in the home of missing person, Penelope Fairfax, twenty, as nurse Helen Malinski, thirty-one. Fairfax is still nowhere to be found, though authorities suspect her professor, Hector Arlington, twenty-nine, to be responsible for her disappearance. According to a report given by her close friend—'" Joy broke off, catching sight of my face.

I put up my hand before she could stutter out an apology or further brace herself for another emotional storm from me. It jangled my nerves to hear that story, but I couldn't muster the energy to be angry with her.

"It's okay, really. Forget about it," I said, somehow void of my usual feelings regarding this sensitive subject.

Joy's lips stayed parted for a moment as she considered how to reply. At last she lowered the screen of her laptop and tried to meet my eyes. "It's…it's not okay, like you said before—" she began, and it was my turn to blush. I tried to object that I had spoken rashly that afternoon, but she overruled me, "No. I understand what it's like to lose someone you love. Nothing ever is the same, you're right about that."

I was stunned at this declaration. I'd grouped her in with all the rest unknowingly, pegging her for one of the insensitive rabble who'd been lucky enough to never be touched by the stinging hand of grief, but I'd been wrong. My shame intensified, but something even deeper inside felt like it had become unhinged and allowed a bottled up, venomous emotion to leak out. It was painful, but it was as if my heart was lanced and a little of the poison it contained had drained out.

"When I was small, I lived with my parents in Kobe. They were both killed in the Hanshin earthquake. I'd been visiting my grandmother in Okinawa that week. I don't remember much of them, because I came to live in California with my aunt and uncle right after they died. But I remember going to their funeral and crying for them. When I got old enough to understand, my uncle finally told me how they died. The true loss of them didn't hit me until then. They were trapped underneath rubble for hours and ended up suffocating. No one could help them, and they couldn't get out." Tears welled up in her eyes, making those dark, inky circles shine even brighter. Her sorrow set my own emotions into a tailspin, too, and I felt my breathing turn aggravated.

"I'm sorry, Joy, If I had...I don't really know what you want me to say."

"I'm not telling you this to try and get sympathy, or anything, Sarah. I just can't stand to sit by and watch someone else suffer alone with their pain like I did. It's wrong to not give kindness where it's needed. That's why I tried to pry the other day. I just want to be there for you, because it doesn't really seem like anyone else is."

I was dumbfounded by her forwardness and insight into what I thought to be the most private sector of my life. My initial reaction was to push her away, to tell her that I appreciated the thought, but I was fine. I opened my mouth with the intent to say it, but the words got stuck in my throat.

I couldn't do it. I just couldn't reject her, because Joy reminded me too much of Lea. They were the same: bleeding hearts, looking for a project. Lea loved a good fixer-upper; she had been surrounded by them. Kids who were having trouble in school, wallflowers that were just a confidence boost away from being popular, and misunderstood off-beats had been Lea's disciples. She had been such a help-a-holic, that she'd successfully transformed her boyfriend, Stephen, from one of the most bullied students in our school to a member of our Winter Formal court.

I had a strong inkling that Joy, too, had a similar addiction of nurturing the downtrodden, and though I intimately understood the inner-workings of her *modus operandi*, I couldn't turn her away. Though I didn't say a word, I managed to look her directly in the eye for the first time that night. From the look she returned, I knew she'd understood that I was going to let her in.

8

TUESDAY AND WEDNESDAY passed in a blur of nervous anticipation. The highlights of my days were my capers in the dining hall. I was on my way to becoming the campus's most infamous milk smuggler, and every evening Felix lapped up the spoils of my thievery with greed.

I went to classes just to keep my head busy, and though I always attempted to do the homework assigned to me, I couldn't seem to focus on anything. After a day or two of ordering Felix to stay locked up in my room, I decided to let him move around campus with me, once he assured me that no one else could see him. He was manic, constantly moving around, chasing things, shaking his head or observing nothing. I'd watch him during the lectures I attended as he floated near the ceiling, ice-skating on air. His apparent madness amused me, but it was also sort of frightening to glean from this behavior just how unhinged and inhuman his mind was.

Nonetheless, he was always captivating to behold. There wasn't a moment that passed when he seemed to be *truly* there, and this fascinated me. I could never concoct a theory about him that didn't seem ludicrous, or settle on just what he was made out of. Ectoplasm seemed like a possibility.

I was pretty sure my classmates and those in my dorm noticed my eyes always tracking what they saw as thin air. No doubt their concerns regarding my sanity increased.

On Thursday morning in the middle of the Core lecture, the first in a series of very peculiar occurrences began. As I was trying to focus on what a fellow student was saying — something ridiculous about hip-hop music being like Walmart — a sharp ringing hummed in both of my ears. The sound grew so loud it blocked out everything else in the room. I tried to make it stop by swallowing and shaking my head to clear my ears.

Felix looked over at me, stopping his midair dance, as still as if he were a painted image rather than a sentient being. The ringing increased, along with my heartbeat. It continued for the rest of my lecture, then faded as suddenly as it had come. When I asked Felix about the incident and his stare, he responded, "I just heard it too. That was all."

That evening, Joy texted asking if we should get together again, this time just to hang out instead of do work. She and her boyfriend, Kyle, were going to take a walk in the woods to the Wishing Tree, and she asked if I wanted to come. I didn't feel like staring at a blank page while telling myself to start my homework, so I agreed to tag along.

It was drizzling, but Joy and I had a decent talk when Kyle wasn't butting in. He seemed to be the sort of person who was desperate to prove his intellectual superiority to anyone in the vicinity. I learned right away he loved correcting trivial mistakes and slips of the tongue in a condescending tone. Scoffs and eye-rolls were his go-to response for anything that a person said, even something as harmless as "Wow, it's cold outside" was met with "Oh, how original", and I couldn't for the life of me figure out what Joy saw in him. I guessed that their relationship was the sort that begins out of a need for comfort and affection when forced into a new environment devoid of close friends or family.

I anticipated the Wishing Tree to leave me feeling as empty as before. Instead, as Joy and Kyle scribbled wishes on scraps of paper, I heard a sound that was like hundreds of soft, slurred voices. My heart picked up tempo as I was assailed by a bundle of emotions, none of which belonged to me. It was like all the feelings, all the longing, aching, hoping, wondering, and hungering that people left by that tree, their wishes surging toward me. Powerful emotions wrapped around me, and my breathing grew laborious.

Joy noticed my hand clawing at my throat and stopped writing. "You okay, Sarah?" she asked with a worried tone, and I tried to offer a convincing smile.

"I'm good, but something just went down the wrong pipe."

Kyle scoffed, a cynical smile spreading across his face. "Hah. I think you mean that you're experiencing *pulmonary aspiration*," he said, raising his eyebrows as if this were common sense.

I stared at him, deadpan, until his sneer faded and he resumed writing his wish.

That night, for the first time since the day the police had come to the door with the news about Lea, I couldn't sleep. Usually for me, sleep was a sanctuary of rest from my hyperactive twin demons of anger and depression. I ran to it willingly and fell into it effortlessly, but that night was different. I tossed and turned for hours, peeking up every so often to see Felix watching me.

"Don't you ever sleep?" I asked him around three in the morning.

He prowled closer, looking thoughtful. "I can. Do you want me to?"

"Well, yeah. It creeps me out how you just sit there and watch me. Quit that, will you?" I requested.

Felix blinked his lantern eyes. "If you say so, Sarah." He curled up and went to sleep without further ado.

Feeling a bit more at ease, I lay my head back on the pillow and sighed. I was beginning to slip away when the sense that Felix was watching me returned. As I glanced over to check, a dark silhouette on the other side of my window startled me. I screamed as the blurred figure that looked like a man with antlers growing out of his head fled from my vision.

Felix sprang awake, his gaze locked on where my shaking finger pointed.

"Wh-what was that thing!?" I hollered, pulling the blankets closer to my chest. "Felix, go see!"

The feline spirit obeyed at once, pushing his head under the curtain and peering out into the night. "There's nothing out there," he said after several tense seconds.

"But you felt it too, didn't you? There was something standing there. You *had* to have felt it." My voice sounded like the shrieking breath of the wind whistling through a crack in the window.

"I'm sorry, Sarah. I was sleeping."

I SLEPT THROUGH my class Friday morning, awaking without a hint of guilt but a great deal of anxiety. One day left. One day until I went back to Unreal City. One day until I was going to enact my plan to see my sister again, even if it was just a projection of my memories of her.

I'd decided I would go through with it, though I'd say nothing to Felix about it beforehand. There were many things I found myself wanting to ask him, but every time I was on the brink of voicing them, a disquiet like the one I'd felt when I'd researched familiar spirits shut my lips for me. I was aware that the answers were there. I just didn't want to know them yet. I didn't think I could handle digesting all this new information at once, so I chose the peace that came along with ignorance, meager as it was.

My afternoon class was almost unbearable. I spent the three-hour period doodling in my notebook, trying to render the scenes I had created in my garden on paper so I wouldn't forget them. My artwork was less than amazing, and I gave up after I noticed that the bear looked more like a walrus. Maybe I'd commission Joy to draw them for me.

The pent up anxiety in me decided to come out in the form of tapping my pencil relentlessly on my notebook until I got a dirty look from the girl sitting beside me, at which point I settled for tracing spirals over and over on the blank paper meant for taking notes. That was something I could draw. Spirals were easy.

Class ended and I bolted from the building. In there, it had been stifling and I'd felt trapped. In there, we'd all been packed together like sausages sealed in plastic. Now I could break away, let the frustration and anger leak out.

One. More. Day. One. More. Day. I repeated these three words in my mind every time my sneakers hit the ground. It became a mantra, until another thought rocked me.

Why not tonight? What's stopping me? The weekend's here, and it's not like I was getting a lot of work done anyway. I'll give Felix my hair tonight.

I stopped on the dirt path that was the long road through the woods back to Merrill, trying to think of a reason not to. As I was considering, a flashing of red and blue lights near the dorms of College Ten caught my eye. Suspicions aroused, I changed direction and slid down the fern-carpeted hillside to get closer. Even from hundreds of feet away, I could tell from the growing commotion that something terrible had happened. Muffled screams came from a crowd gathering around a parked police car and ambulance. I craned my neck to see what manner of calamity had occurred, and caught a glimpse of a stretcher being unloaded from the back of the ambulance.

"What's going on?" I demanded of a tall, lanky student obstructing my view.

He didn't look down as he answered. "A body was found. I heard them say he must've been there since last night. I can't believe it took this long."

"What?" I breathed, pushing past him. I had to know exactly what had happened, who had died, and how. I didn't understand why it mattered so much then, but I've come to realize that it was my built up regret that I hadn't been there the night they found Lea, Stephen, and Isaac. I'd played out that scene in my head so many times, finding it suitable punishment for my absence. The concerned onlookers, the police sirens. I'd imagined in that scene that I would push through the crowd to find her there, and I suppose that rehearsed frustration had been enough to make me struggle forward when this uncannily similar incarnation presented itself.

As I peered around a girl's shoulder, I steeled myself, bracing to see any number of awful things—blood, burn wounds, or broken bones. Nothing could have prepared me for what it actually was.

My stomach tightened as I caught sight of the dead boy's face, sallow yellow in color, the skin tight but bloated underneath. His lips and eyelids were tinged blackish-blue and a stillness that could only be death had settled over his body.

Something akin to a very intense form of carsickness gripped me, and I felt a scream bubble up from inside and escape. I grabbed at the girl nearest to me, unable to control myself.

"Get off me!" she grunted, trying to break free from my grasp as I clung tighter.

The paramedics were trying to block the scene from view and disperse the crowd, but I could see it all. He had been laid behind a building in the center of campus. They lifted the dead boy's body, and the sight of his stiffened and lifeless limbs turned my grip vice-like. The girl was screaming, and her friend pried me off with tremendous effort as tears slid down my face.

"How did he die?" I gasped, the reeling in my head causing me to stumble. I could feel the gaze of the crowd shifting to watch me now. "How did he die?" I repeated louder, my tears flowing with abandon.

No one answered, but I didn't care. All I could do was stare. The meat of his throat was bulging as if it were saturated with water. And dear God, that skin. Yellow. Black. Blue. The form of a human being desecrated by the onset of rot already creeping in. But it wouldn't have acted this quickly. His lips must have turned black *as* he died.

"*HOW DID HE DIE?*" I shrieked, looking from face to frightened face, pleading with them, begging them. I reached out for another arm to hold onto and everyone backed away. A policeman was coming toward me, unsmiling. "*God, someone tell me! PLEASE!*"

My unbalanced behavior elicited a reply at last: "He drowned!"

FROM THAT MOMENT until I woke up hours later in the Student Health Center with a pounding headache, my memory is blank. Disoriented, I cried out, and a nurse came by to inform me that I had fainted. I tried to get my bearings, and noticed with horror there was an IV drip in my arm.

"Did you drug me?" I demanded.

"Just something to calm you. When they brought you in, they said you were pretty frantic. Now could you answer these questions for me, sweetie?"

She went on, exploring my health history, asking personal questions and recommending I speak with the mental health counselor. I didn't pay attention. My thoughts were haunted by the memories of the drowned boy. He'd been found in the middle of campus. Miles away from any bodies of water. Just the way Lea had been left.

I didn't know what to do. I didn't know who to call or who to talk to. Should I alert the police? Wouldn't they connect the cases? How could this be happening here, of all places? Sure, Monterey was close, but it was too much of a coincidence. It sickened me to entertain the thought that I was somehow connected.

After I'd passed the gauntlet of paperwork and prying queries, I requested to be released on the basis that I was not ill, and the staff complied with obvious reluctance. I fled the health center, finding myself wanting to talk to Felix more than anyone else. Perhaps because he was my own imaginary friend, and being completely insane himself, I knew he wouldn't judge me. Or abandon me. I still don't know why that thought comforted me that night.

Students were hanging out in the hall, but went silent as I trudged by, my head down and hood up. I couldn't get the image of the dead flesh of the boy out of my mind. It was stuck there, following me like the moon follows a traveler making his way down the road in the night.

Lea probably looked like that when they found her. Just like that. Black. Yellow. Blue. I tried my best not to apply that condition to the memory of my sister's face.

I burst into my dorm room and shut the door behind me to find Felix sitting placidly on my bed, staring at a corner of the ceiling. I was about to speak when something about that corner caught my attention, too. The longer I looked at it, the dizzier I felt, though there was nothing there to be seen. I felt a rising sense of anxiety — a feeling of something buried, something trapped. I shook this off and brought my attention back to the matter at hand.

"Felix. Someone on campus died today. They were murdered. In the same way my sister was," I informed him. I don't know what I expected from him, but he only blinked.

"Terrible news. I'm sorry to hear that," he said, and sounded like he almost meant it.

My breathing grew agitated, and I fiddled with my necklace in frustration. I was pacing now, back and forth across the small space between the desks and the bunk beds.

"Does this feel like it's connected to you? 'Cause it does to me," I cried, unable to articulate the core of what I was feeling but trying to get some sort of ball rolling in my mind.

"Could be. I can't say for sure. I wasn't there," Felix said, and I glared at him.

"Are you always this goddamn vague?" I retorted and his needle-lined grin widened, pleased by my aggravation.

"Constantly and without exception," he cooed.

I sighed and tried to think of what and how to ask him, remembering Mama Stella's warnings about the familiar spirits. After a moment of going over her words in my head, something echoed at the back of my mind: *It's what the man in the library call it, so most of us Cunning Folk come to call it that too.*

"Felix, who did Mama Stella mean when she talked about the 'man at the library?'"

Felix perked up. "One of the Cunning Folk. His garden looks like a library and he seems to be well-connected with the others," he told me. "He's not very friendly, but he never turns down a conversation with one of the Cunning Folk. He seems to want to study you people."

"And if I told this man what was happening to me, do you think he might be able to help me?" It was a shot in the dark, but at least it was a shot.

"Perhaps, if he's in. He seems to be around most of the time, though, so chances are pretty good." Felix's whine was starting to sound hopeful, and he studied my hair with wide eyes.

I was about to give it to him when another thought occurred to me. "Can—can I die in Unreal City?"

"No. Not your body, anyway," Felix said and I raised an eyebrow.

"What do you mean? Tell me everything I need to know to stay safe there," I commanded, hoping that wording was proper enough to get a straight answer out of him.

"You cannot be physically harmed there, but when you are in another garden, you are under the complete control of the one who owns it. Should the person catch you and hold you there, and should they be a particularly unsavory person, they could submit you to any number of awful things. And they will all seem real. And you will remember them as real. If they are especially creative, you could lose your mind. Whatever psychological stress your consciousness endures there will remain when you return to this side of reality," he explained and the pit that was sinking in my stomach plunged deeper.

"But that's rare, right? That hardly happens, I'm sure?" That might've been the reason the boy who'd wandered into my garden had run when he first saw me. He had no idea who I was or if I could be trusted.

"Not as rare as you'd think. That City does strange things to people's minds. The combination of human nature and unchecked power generally produces disaster," Felix said, delighted at the notion.

So if I did go see the man at the library, I'd have to hope he was of the sane and merciful variety, and if I did choose to create a shade that looked like my sister, I'd have to hope it wouldn't be the first step down the road to total insanity. I sank into the computer chair, tormented by the possibilities of these dangers.

But I had come this far. Stopping now seemed impossible.

"All right, Felix," I said, reaching for the scissors in my desk drawer. "Let's go back."

9

GETTING THERE WAS easier this time. I didn't get
stuck on my way up. The brief period of blankness separating
the two sides of reality faded without delay and I awoke in the
autumnal forest I'd created during my last visit to Unreal City.
The heightened perception flooded back into my mind, and I
flexed my fingers, shuddering at the unlimited possibilities. As
I looked around the clearing with its whispering shower of red
and orange leaves, I itched to start weaving different fantasies,
but held off for now. I didn't know how much time I had, so
they would have to wait until I saw the man at the library. Lea
would have to wait.

I ran my fingers over the lock of shortened hair I'd clipped.
Felix trotted to my side, a spring in his step. He'd swallowed it
up so voraciously, almost nipping my fingertip in the process.
I stepped in the direction of the lane, stopping when I saw Felix
bristle. His eyes grew wide.

"Someone's coming. Someone knows you've just arrived,"
he told me, and I looked wildly around, waiting for my visitor
to become visible.

"Who is it? Can you tell?" I asked, creeping closer to Felix. "Felix, can you fight? Can you hurt people?"

"I can, but only if you order me to. In this world I can trap or trick, and in the other I can injure or kill," he explained, his confidence mixed with the nonchalant willingness to take a life both reassuring me and making my blood run cold. "But we won't need to, right now. It's Angus."

The face of the boy I'd seen before appeared over the top of the hill, his warm brown eyes studying me. We looked each other over until Felix broke the silence.

"Hello, Aodh," Felix called into the woods. The boy looked over his shoulder, a little panicked, but something he saw caused his shoulders to relax.

"Hello, Pan. Or is it still Aoife?" asked a deep, resonating voice from the trees.

"My name is Felix now, old friend," my familiar spirit said to the trees. "I have a new master."

"Yes, Stella told us about you," the boy said, and I was surprised to hear his accent was Scottish. "She said your name is Sarah. Is that right?"

"Yeah," I said, still defensive. "And you're Angus."

"I am," he said, sliding closer to me, his body language revealing he did not trust me.

It struck me as peculiar how careful he was being. I wondered if I looked like the type of person who would try to harm a stranger. Looking past the boy, I realized who Felix had been talking to. On the trunks of the trees, a face had appeared in the wrinkles on the wood. It looked like a warping of the wood, but I could sense a palpable knot of energy humming around it. The expression in the tree was one of melancholy, but not quite pain; if it were a human face it would have looked thousands of years old. Hanging from the branches on either side of the face, two glass lanterns had appeared, both alight with a dancing blue flame.

Angus looked as if he was trying to say something, but just couldn't get it out. My annoyance threshold had been surpassed.

"You know, I'm not a psychopath, okay? I'm not gonna hurt you, so you can nut up and stop quivering like a child already."

He started a little at my verbal assault. "You're definitely not what I expected," he stammered, running his fingers through his shaggy hair.

I raised an eyebrow, refusing to let up on him. "And what is that supposed to mean?" I hated people who got under my skin, and he was definitely doing that. I hate letting them get away with ruffling my feathers unless I've given them a suitable ruffling in return.

"I-I don't know, I really can't say. I'm sorry for running off the other day. I just—this place. Got to be careful, you ken what I mean?" he tried to appeal to me.

When his defensive look faded away, he was quite handsome, in a rugged way. That irked me even more, and I narrowed my eyes at him.

"No, I don't *ken* what you mean," I shot back, guessing very well from the context what he was trying to say, but wanting to give him a hard time regardless. He stared at me for a moment.

"So it's true what they say about Americans, then?"

"What?"

"That you're all soft in the head?" His smile was devilish, and irritation shuddered through me.

"Ah, nothing says 'trust me' like good old fashioned bigotry." I turned on my heel and walked toward the end of my garden. "Now, laddie, if ye dinnae mind, I'll be off!" I mocked in a poor attempt to ridicule his accent.

He laughed it off and followed me. I gave him a sidelong glance and kept going.

"God, you are a feisty one, aren'tcha?" His laugh was loud and clear. "Don't get upset. I'm only teasing. Where are you off to?"

"To see someone in another garden. A man at a library," I said, not slowing my walk.

He whistled. "Going to see creepy Arthur? Hoo! And alone, too? Well, if anyone's got answers, it'll be him, *but,* well, I guess we all make mistakes when we first get here. Though I'm surprised it's taken you so little time to go wandering. Usually people stay and enjoy themselves a bit longer before they go roving. What's the rush, eh?"

Something about his interest suggested an ulterior motive, and I wondered whether I should be honest with him.

"I want to ask him something. Things are—are weird for me right now. I need to talk to someone who knows the way things work around here, and I thought he might know how to help me," I told Angus as we approached the barrier. I prepared to cross over, but he grabbed me by the shoulder. I turned to face him, irked that he had the nerve to touch me.

"Listen, don't take this the wrong way, but you're kind of an idiot—"

"*Excuse me?*"

"I was going to say—" he shouted over me, "—I was going to say an idiot about the way things run here. We all are when we first get here! It's not your fault. I've been here since I was a kid, and I've seen things, some not-so-nice things, happen to nice young ladies like yourself. Things that were easily preventable. Arthur's a strange sort of guy. So could you shelf your pride for a day and let me come with you to see him?" he requested.

I considered this, then turned up my nose. "I think I can manage on my own, thanks," I said and took another step.

"Well, if you say so." He turned and headed in the other direction. "But you're going the wrong way."

I stopped and looked down at Felix, who affirmed with a nod that Angus was right. I swiveled back around.

"All right, show me the way," I instructed without apology and Angus laughed again, that high, airy sound.

"Ah, so she's not a lost cause, Aodh! We'll have to work on that attitude, though," he said with a grin, gesturing for me to come near him. I did so reluctantly. "Well, we can walk, but that'll have us tromping through everyone else's garden. You generally want to steer clear of Poe's. That's a rule around here. Not even Stella goes there." Before I could ask who Poe was, he raised his hand. "So generally, we like to take the airways. This is your garden, missy, so would you kindly do us the honor?"

"Of?"

"Make something that can fly," he said, looking skeptical I didn't think of this myself.

I heard Felix, walking near my ankles, give a murmuring laugh and I narrowed my gaze at the two of them. Aodh remained silent and frozen behind us, observing. Turning my eyes on him, I focused on thinking of something that could get us airborne and decided a magic carpet would work as well as anything. I willed it into being, and it materialized in a swirl of golden fragments. I took command and sat down cross-legged at the front, Felix slinking up under my arm until he rested on my thigh. Angus sat down behind us, chuckling under his breath.

"Isn't your familiar coming?" I asked and Angus shook his head.

"He'll be there when we get there. Aodh isn't like the others. He lives inside of things. He'll be inside the walls, listening," Angus reassured me. I didn't quite know what he meant by this. "Now fly us up past the reaches of your garden and we'll be able to look down on the City."

I did as he said, gripping the edges of the fine Persian rug and lifting us off the ground. We climbed aloft, going higher and higher, until the trees became toy models and we pierced through the boundary that was the ceiling of my garden.

It was a very different view of Unreal City. I had to send the carpet to a staggering height to see it all, and discovered that this world was flat. Each garden was a segment on a disc, with what looked like a white spoke in the center of them all. The City rotated at an almost imperceptible pace, surrounded on every side by a field of stars. I marveled at the sight.

"Who owns this place up here?" I was so caught up in my wonderment I'd forgotten to be rude to Angus.

"No one. It's a free-for-all in the airway. I can even drive now, watch," Angus said and the carpet lurched forward without my command. We fought over control of it for a moment before he relinquished it to me, chuckling as if he found it all very amusing. I scoffed at his light-heartedness. The poisonous feeling the corpse on campus had left me with hadn't faded, and kept my foul mood going strong.

"So, blondie, how is it that you came to find that spirit of yours?" Angus asked me as we swooped over the various gardens. I could see Blanche's, and in it some hundreds of feet below I saw her playing in the meadow.

"He found me. He said he'd been following me...why were you following me, Felix?"

My familiar moved his shoulders in what looked like a shrug. "I look for those who seem to want to leave this world the most. You were reeking of misery."

His answer didn't please or satisfy me, but it sent Angus into another round of snickering.

"Why do you care anyway? How did you come to be here?" I turned the focus to him. I drifted over an urban garden that must've been Angus's since it neighbored my own, then a swampy garden with a bayou I presumed belonged to Mama Stella.

"Ah, for the love of—you're *still* going the long way. Well, we've gone too far now...Let me drive," he complained. I gave him a dirty look, but allowed him control of the carpet. "As for me, I sort of stumbled into this place. I live out in the highlands, and when I was lad, I went wandering out too far one day and got lost inside of a wood. Aodh was there, and I talked with him a while. I kept going back, and eventually he offered me the *deal*. I was too young to think twice, and now—now well, I don't know anything else but this life," he said, sounding almost sorry.

"You say that like it's a bad thing. Isn't this place a dream come true?" I asked with genuine confusion.

Angus gave a dry, barking laugh. "It's as much a blessing as it is a curse. You'll find out soon enough, I'm sure," he said cryptically, then made a noise of interest and pointed downward. "That there's Ranjit's garden. He's also a bit of a rotten soul. You'll probably want to stay away from there, too."

Angus flew low so I could see. This garden was submerged in water, and under the waves I saw a connecting series of structures that appeared similar to diving bells. In the water, a creature that looked like a cross between a dolphin and a goat swam around an illuminated window, lashing its tail about and shaking its horned head. On its sides were patches of light that were evocative of the markings of the bioluminescent fishes of the deep sea.

"He's your classic megalomaniac. Fancies himself a king, and 'governs' a realm that I'm certain Caligula would find a touch distasteful. He's dirt poor on the real side of things, however, though he'll hardly admit it," Angus commented with the air of a tour guide passing a famous sight-seeing spot.

Zooming past Ranjit's sea, we passed a village that looked like a Mexican pueblo with beautiful hanging lanterns lighting the street-ways in an array of vibrant colors.

"The woman who stays there is hardly ever in, but I think her name is Jezebel. Not sure, really," Angus said without interest, pushing us onward over a barren garden that was mostly blanketed by clouds streaming with electricity.

At last we arrived at a garden with gray skies and a massive tower stretching up to meet us. We circled it on our way down, landing at the bland entranceway. The plants, ground, trees, and front of the building were nondescript and appeared to be bleached of color. Angus stepped off the carpet gingerly and left it lying in front of the steps leading up to the tower. I followed, craning my neck to take it all in.

"And *this*," Angus sighed, "is Arthur's library."

We scaled the steps without speaking. Any hint of a cheery mood Angus had been trying to inject into our interactions was wiped away when we pushed open the front doors. The doors were functional—no attempt at ornamentation, like something you'd find at an airport, and with all the charm of a DMV. Inside, I was surprised to find much of the same atmosphere. Quiet rooms padded by concrete or plastic walls, grey, coarse carpet with unimaginative neutral designs. Fluorescent light bulbs lit the room, creating a washed out, industrial look. The smell of paper and glue hung in the air.

We glanced in the first room off the entrance. It was packed, every available space filled with books, each shelf catalogued according to standard library protocol. The reference books were on this floor, and two book-lined hallways led to more rooms that looked the same. At the very end of the main cavernous hall with its silent compilations of histories, facts, and stories, was an olive green elevator.

Angus walked to it and pressed the button, then stepped back and rocked on his heels. Felix and I joined him and waited, and I sensed the energy of Aodh's spirit approaching. He was sidling through the pages of the books, down through the wooden shelves, and up into the walls. I could see him sometimes, always with the twin blue lights — sometimes in the lights overhead, sometimes gleaming in the golden foil on the covers of the books.

We boarded the elevator, no one daring to break the humming quiet of that stifled space. After the doors closed and we were faced with a choice of 140 different floors, Angus asked the ceiling, "Aodh, which floor is he on? Can you tell?"

"Thirty-seven," came an electrical response from the elevator speaker — Aodh, speaking through the faux sound-system of this construct.

Angus stabbed the button with his pointer finger and it shot upward, making my stomach go woozy. My ears filled with pressure then popped as we came to a bobbing halt at floor thirty-seven. The doors sprang open with a cheerless little *ding* and Angus led the way out with Felix trotting behind him, his tail high in the air. I stalked out behind them, keeping my shoulders straight and my head high. Whoever this Arthur was, I didn't want him to see that I was discomfited by his colorless world.

We rounded a grouping of shelves to see a stocky little man with glasses lying on a leather fainting couch, his head resting on a pile of what looked like dictionaries. His arms were folded across his chest, and a few inches above his face floated a book. With a nod of his head, the page turned on its own.

He must have heard us coming, and drawled something in an accent that sounded Russian, not bothering to look up. The man's hair was a patchy, graying blond, and his pale face had splotches of red on its paunchy cheeks. Bright blue eyes shone behind his glasses, and dark red lips slick as liver curled as he spoke.

"Just coming to ask a few questions, Arthur," Angus interrupted in a voice I assumed he meant to sound light-hearted or casual, yet came out sounding anxious.

The bespectacled man looked up with little interest, caught sight of Felix and me, and sprang off the couch. He flew into a panic, lifting the voluminous coat he wore and spinning around in place. As he turned, his whole body changed shape, stretching out, getting taller and leaner in seconds. His hair grew long, sleek, and lustrous. When he faced us again, he looked decades younger: his features were sharp, delicate, and breathtakingly handsome. His clothes were smart, elegant and fitted, and thin half-moon glasses sat on his nose. The eyes, however, had remained the same: that cold, startling blue.

"Of course, Angus, you are welcome here at any time," he said, his reedy voice transformed into a deep, arresting tone saturated in affected kindness.

However attractive he appeared now, the knowledge of his true appearance disturbed me. I wish he would've stayed ugly.

"May I present Sarah, our newest addition? She's the one who's got all the questions, actually," Angus said, swooping out of the way and waving his wide, bony hand in my direction.

Arthur's eyebrows lifted and he eased over to me, both hands extended. He took my unoffered palm in his and closed his fingers around it.

"Welcome, dear girl. Welcome to the Unreal City. How many times have you been here now?" he asked, warmth and lust vying for control in his voice. A wave of revulsion trickled down my spine.

"Um, two," I grunted and extricated my hand from his, resisting the urge to wipe it on my pants.

"And what is it that you'd like to ask me? I'd be happy to oblige, my dear," Arthur continued, waving Angus and I toward a pair of seats that he drew out of thin air.

Tentatively we sat down and Felix curled his tail around my foot, standing at attention between Arthur and me. The librarian pulled his couch closer to the chairs with a curl of his fingers and assumed a lounging position on it. He looked at me expectantly.

I had no idea how to begin. The pressure from the anticipating ears of Angus, Arthur, and, from the walls, Aodh, made me freeze up. I looked away from their faces and down to Felix for help, realizing I had no idea how to phrase my predicament or why I'd thought it would be a good idea to come here.

Eventually I decided that I'd better just explain what happened to both of them. Though I felt exposed explaining the death of my sister and my happening across the corpse on campus to complete strangers, it felt cathartic to say it out loud. Angus's face contorted in pain when I got to the poignant moments of my story, and though I tried to always police my emotions, seeing him react made me want to cry. Arthur's face, however, remained still and unfeeling during the entire duration of my tale. When I'd at last finished, he rubbed his chin and thought for a moment.

"I am not sure what it is you'd like me to tell you, Miss Sarah," Arthur said at last.

I looked blankly at him. "Well, I don't know either, to be honest. I just find it all very — odd. It seems like a bit too much of a coincidence, don't you think? I just don't want to be that kind of idiot that ends up dead because I let everything just happen around me," I tried to explain, starting to feel embarrassed that I'd even come here in the first place.

Arthur made a tutting noise. "I suppose I can see where you are coming from, though I lament your lack of direction," he said, and the comment stung. He lifted his hand into the air and tilted his head backward. "Grimoire, come over here," he commanded.

A rushing of wind came from the back of the library and a large tome flew forth. Both the front and back cover were set with a sculpture of a face, each of them identical, their eyes glowing eerily with the light that I took to be the life-force of each of the familiars. It whisked its way over Arthur's head and landed neatly in his hands, the pages fluttering as he fingered through them. He licked his fingers every time he turned a page, something that made me bristle as the sound of his dampened finger scraped against the dry paper.

"You heard what she said. Show me, Grimoire. Send me in the right direction," he murmured to the book, and stopped without any apparent reason at a page of his choosing. His eyes scanned the words written there.

I just couldn't sit back and watch anymore. "Just tell me if I'm safe or not. Tell me what's doing this. Tell me what's happening," I pleaded.

Arthur looked at me, his eyes scolding, like I was an impudent child acting out of line. I looked to Angus for assistance, only to see that he had disappeared, along with the presence of Aodh. Arthur tracked my gaze, and his painted-on smile broadened with real satisfaction.

"He has gone, child. His time here has run out," Arthur said, not without a touch of delight. My hand went unconsciously to Felix's neck and I felt his fur shiver under my touch. "I don't think I can explain so easily the peculiar turn your life has taken. I think perhaps everyone looks for a reason when their lives are torn apart. It is natural to want something to blame. But I cannot say for certain that the reason behind your sister's death is related to your admittance into Unreal City."

I was downtrodden and infuriated by the answer, but I kept my face straight. I didn't feel brave enough to test this man. "But I daresay, my girl," he continued, "that you are in need of information far more basic than this. I fear that no one has given you the perspective that you need about this place."

"What?" I breathed.

"Have you given it blood yet?" he asked, folding lean fingers over his knees.

I blinked at Felix, who refused to meet my gaze, then back at him. "Felix? My familiar?"

"Yes, you silly girl. I am speaking English, aren't I? My perception hasn't shifted that far, I hope," Arthur said, clearly agitated. At my side, Felix was growling in that low, catlike rumble, as if he were threatening Arthur to stay quiet.

"No, no I haven't. Does something bad happen if I do?" My voice was trembling now. Arthur leaned his head onto his hand, his white-blue eyes startling me.

"You still have a chance to break away from here, if you can. You can tempt the familiars with other things — other parts perhaps, but until you've given them the blood, you can still bid them leave you forever. Once they taste it, they'll be bound to you for the rest of your life," he said and moistened his lips, his breathing ragged.

My heart rate was skyrocketing as I tried to unpack what all of this meant. "Wait, wait. Why would I want to break away? Isn't this place a paradise?" I could hardly contain my panic at what he might be about to reveal. Behind those cold eyes, I could see the bank of fog that was his antisocial, nearly sociopathic nature start to clear. His faux-face almost became human at that moment, as if he were remembering a flash from another life — a time of warmth and feelings of love, and the very moment it all came crashing down.

"This is a prison," he said, lips trembling.

"But you have whatever you want, you have —" I looked around to find a word to classify this bizarre sanctuary, "full access to all the knowledge you could ever want."

"I am trapped by my unending desire. I return here whenever possible, spending an eternity turning through pages upon pages. I could devise better ways of getting it into my head, but I choose not to. It's just too painfully satisfying the way it is. I've read every book on the floors below me and I can't stop now. Not until I reach the top. My life on the other side is a nightmare. This is my only stable reality," he rasped, his expression desperate. "And do you know the worst thoughts that come to me now? The ones that stab me in my brief moments of clarity?"

"Wh-what?"

"This has only been in my head. I know this library isn't limited by my own knowledge, but I'm not even sure if any of what I've been reading is accurate to reality. I'm too afraid to even find out. I'm not even sure how long it's *been* since I came here—" he stopped himself abruptly and put his hand delicately over his mouth, as if he'd been acting indecently and only just realized. "I apologize, miss. It's just... It's been so long since anyone's been here, so long since I've talked to anyone, or told anybody about this—I lost myself momentarily. For-give me."

I almost got up to leave at that moment, but I was greedy for more knowledge. Or maybe I just figured that I'd rather face the risk of getting trapped inside this sad, shattered man's darkest dreams than get trapped inside my own. He regained his composure, but still cleared his throat several times.

"Listen to me carefully. They hunt the ones who are tempted the most by their offer. They wait in places where deep energy once flowed. It sustains them until they find their prey, and then they strike. The things that this world can create are wonderful, but it will forever alter your connection with the reality we were born into, and do not think for a moment that you will be able to overcome it. I have seen people make it work for them. Angus is one of the stronger ones, I think because he was so young when he first came here, it became a part of his development. But this City is not to be toyed with. Think before you give him blood, and if you can resist—if you can go forward and live your life and abandon the eternal ach-ing remembrance of something that pushed the boundaries of sensory wonder, you will have won. But once he goes away, he will be gone for all time," Arthur warned.

"Thank you. Thank you for telling me," I breathed. Our eyes connected for a moment and the longer I grew used to his beautiful mask, the sicker my stomach felt. I was forgetting his true appearance. It was working.

"I fear I cannot tell you anything about the strange events that have befallen you and though I doubt that—" he stopped and his eyebrows lifted as if something had just occurred to him. "Wait...I wonder." Arthur snapped his fingers and Grimoire lifted upward. "Take me back to my three last memories of Charles Poe," he commanded his familiar. His eyes glazed as he stared at the pages of the book, the muscles in his face growing lax. Grimoire's pages continued to blow by like an endless flipbook and he stayed in that state for some time. I wondered if I shouldn't just get up and leave while he was still hypnotized, but remained fidgeting in my seat until he came back.

"What happened?" I asked him when he finally blinked.

"I was only just revisiting a few memories to confirm something," he told me, "and my guess was correct. Another one of the Cunning Folk, a man called Charles Poe, inhabitant of the eighth garden, mentioned something similar to your circumstances the last time he came here. He came to me in a panic, saying people were dying around him, that he felt something was chasing him—but I wouldn't take anything he says too seriously. He's deeply disturbed. Insane."

I remembered that name from earlier—Poe. Angus had warned me to stay away from his garden at all costs, and now I supposed I knew why. No matter how you looked at it, wandering through the violent manifestation of a broken mind would be dangerous. I wanted desperately to know what was happening around me—whether I was in danger of losing my life or if the reason my sister had been robbed of hers had been more than a random act of depravity. However, as I sat there intimidated by this husk of a man, I searched inward for the line where courage ended and recklessness began.

"I think I can use that. You've done me a favor, Arthur. You have my thanks," I told him, standing up.

A look of sorrow crossed his face and he jumped to his feet. "Going so soon?" he asked, taking my arm and gently tugging me back down. I resisted him.

"Y-yeah, I've got stuff to do. Sorry," I shrugged, and his face sagged.

"Please, miss, won't you join me for a while longer? I'd like to talk with you more, just a little conversation. I—I can create something wonderful for you, a warm drink, perhaps? A lovely view of the ocean for us to watch? I'd so love to tell you about all the marvelous things I've learned in my time here in the library. I think you might be interested. You might even find them *helpful*," he entreated. If he hadn't frightened me, I would have found him pathetic.

"I'm sorry, but I've really got to go."

"But you *will* come back soon, won't you? You will come visit again?" he clutched at his chest, not bothering to hide his willfulness. The look in his eyes almost broke my heart.

"I will. If I decide to come back to this City at all, that is," I told him firmly, and I wanted to mean it. "Thank you again."

He called goodbyes after me for as long as he could.

10

AS WE EXITED the tower and walked into the grey courtyard outside, I found it hard to speak to Felix.

"How come you never told me any of that stuff before? About the blood?" I asked at last, and he smiled back unflinchingly.

"You never *asked*," he said, much as a child would answer the same question. "I can't tell you anything unless you ask."

"Right," I snapped. I was pretty sure he had already proven he possessed enough liberty to bend that rule and warn me. Sensing his stubbornness, I gave up and decided to take us home, but my thoughts would not become reality. Then I remembered I had no power in other people's gardens.

"So how do I get out of here without disturbing the others if I can't fly?"

"You can only run. Or I can run for you," he offered. When I cocked my head, nonplussed, he grew still and a look of concentration came over his face. At once he grew in size, stretching taller, but retaining almost the same girth. As his legs began to grow freakishly long and skinny, he prompted me to climb atop his back before he became too tall for me to reach.

I did, gripping his cylindrical midsection, no wider than a foot across, as we rose higher into the air. His head was so far away from me he had to bend backward to inform me we were about to move. I curled my arms and legs around him, feeling his stretched spine bump and jostle me as we set into motion, his feet nearly a hundred feet below.

To watch him move was like something out of the most surreal of dreams, but I was more concerned with not falling off. Felix's speed increased with every step, and within a minute we were tearing through the gardens at a pace that would've made my eyes stream in reality. In the middle of our jaunt, I was surprised to encounter another man, grizzled and wearing a long coat, riding in the opposite direction. Our eyes met and in the second I got to look at him, I saw he rode a familiar that looked like a filthy old kelpie. He shot past us as the horse-like spirit pierced through the air and disappeared.

Within minutes we were back in my garden. The feeling of all-powerfulness returned to me and I was comforted. Felix collapsed back to his normal length with a popping and snapping of his bones and a mad rolling of his eyes. I wasn't sure if he was in pain or not, and frankly I was a little too put-off to ask.

Back to his normal size, he looked to me for direction. "Now what shall we do, Sarah? Should we play like we did before? We could explore underground caverns, or swim under the ocean until we find the very bottom, or perhaps catch fireflies, or—"

"No…this time I want to try something a little different." Now that the moment was here, I felt stiff, trying to remember why I'd wanted this at all. It would just bring back all the terrible feelings, rip them through the wound that I'd been trying my best to sew shut every day. But the desire to see her again—to talk to her, even if it wasn't really her—I couldn't resist the temptation. A photo of her wasn't enough. My memories weren't enough. A huge part of my life had been torn away from me, and it wasn't fair. And why should I even try to play fair with a fate that was this cruel? I took a breath and prepared to summon her from the Earth.

I focused all my energy into the soil beneath my feet. Before my eyes the autumnal scene blew away as if by a great gust of wind, and in its place sprouted up a green forest. Vines curled, wildflowers blossomed, towering pines creaked, and moss spread out beneath my feet like a carpet. The longer I focused, pouring out all my love and longing and memories of her life, the hotter the energy around me grew. It was curling around, growing larger and healthier from the nutrients in the soil and the green world above it. The longer I poured that light energy into the ground, the weaker I began to feel. When I could no longer expend anything more, I stumbled back. I panted, feeling everything that I remembered about my sister pulsing in the ground before me, incubating with every beat of its artificial heart.

At once I regretted my choice, and turned back to face Felix. He must have known what I was doing, and I wondered if it would amuse him—but nervousness had replaced his glimmering smile. Burning eyes were fixed on the ground where Lea was, which had begun pulsating gently. He turned toward me, defeat in his eyes.

"Sarah, why did you do this?" he lamented, sounding broken-hearted.

"I just wanted to see her again!" I cried.

In response Felix hunched to the ground, resting his head on his paws as a look of deep sadness passed over his too-human face. He shut his eyes and remained there, still as stone.

Before I could object to his leaving me to deal with this uncertain situation on my own, the ground behind me began to rumble. I turned just in time to see it split apart as a head of blonde hair rose, speckled with fragments of dirt and roots. She came up from the earth, straight backed and smiling, dressed in the clothes I'd last seen her in. Her eyes were there, Lea's eyes — the ones that looked just like mine, except with her own unique softness behind them.

I let out a wail, a desperate mixture of anguish and joy. I'd forgotten how beautiful she was — how healthy and put-together she'd always looked. I stumbled forward when, at last, she had completely risen out of the ground and stood upon her mound of disturbed soil. She was serene, silent, a delicate and unassuming smile on her lips.

"Lea. Lea, say something to me," I begged, resisting the urge to leap forward and take her into my arms.

"Sarah, I missed you."

I ran forward then and pulled her into a tight embrace. It was all there: the smell of the shampoo she always used, the length and texture of her hair, her bony shoulders. She was back with me, she was safe. I could see her again and touch her. We could laugh together again and the raw, aching pain that up until now had never let me rest would be nothing but an unpleasant memory. This would become the real world and that other terrible place would be the nightmare that I only visited briefly to keep my body alive and pay the price for my unending bliss.

"Oh God, Lea. Lea it's you. You're back with me. You can't ever go again. You don't know what it's been like without you," I murmured into her shoulder, laying my head upon her collarbone. I felt her wrap her arms around my waist and hold tight, but there was something mechanical in her response.

I opened my streaming eyes, my heart feeling like someone was twisting it around until all the muscles threatened to fall apart with the tension. I leaned deeper into her and felt the solidness of her chest give way a little. I let go at once and drew back in horror, spotting a crushed depression where my head had been.

"*Lea!*" I wailed, wanting to reach out for her again, but afraid my grip might crush more of her.

Her expression never changed. She was still calm and smiling, but as I watched her, more of her flesh collapsed inward. Her cheeks sunk in, her bones crumpled forward, and the skin around her neck began to shrivel up.

I could hear myself screaming as I fell to my knees. The black, filthy yellow of necrosis crawled across her as she continued to implode. Her blue eyes were eaten by rot for minute after excruciating minutes, until she had become nothing but a clean, pearly skeleton continuing to stand upright before me.

I howled as I cowered on the ground, unable to tear my eyes from the odious sight. As her bones stood poised, the plants around her feet began to stir. Rapidly they snaked and curled around the bones, reaching up to claim her. A tree sprouted from below, pushing her skeleton upward. In seconds she was cocooned inside of the hollowed tree trunk, just a pillar lifting into the air, draped in soil, bark, vines, leaves, grass, and flowers. The lichens and spongy moss attached themselves to her bones and grew around Lea's cleaned corpse, until she had become part of the plant system of my garden. Yet the human shape remained visible as the tree grew only a few feet higher than me. Out of her eye sockets grew two white flowers, and even then I felt as if she were watching me.

I lay upon the mossy ground, sobbing, and the plants grew over my body too, curling around my wrists and through my hair. Flowers fluttered up around my couch of damp flora. Peering through my tears, I could see Felix had gone. I couldn't feel him anywhere, so I lay back on the ground and let myself weep until my senses were almost numb. I couldn't remember when it started happening, but all too late I became aware that the plants were pulling me downward into the plot of churned soil from where the artificial Lea had quickened. I screamed, trying to fight the plant life, but it had grown too tightly around me. I was going into the ground whether I wanted to or not.

I shut my eyes and willed it to stop, to have my garden return to my absolute control, but it would not obey. My feet went under first, and not even the most violent of kicks would slow that downward pull. I was hiccoughing now, trying to claw my way out of the sinking hole, but my fingers only tore through soft soil. I rolled onto my stomach as the vines curled around my torso, and felt my shoulders get swallowed by the ground. The light was starting to fade. There was dirt in my throat, choking me, stinging my eyes and worming its way into my ears. I was being buried alive, going deeper by the minute, and feeling my heart thunder inside of me against the oppressive, smashing force of the earth. Weight pressed in from all sides and I lost the ability to breathe or see. I was suspended, frozen and suffocating in the blackness of this subterranean trap. The voice of Arthur reverberated around in my skull.

This is a prison.

I wanted to scream, I wanted to fight, but my throat was blocked up with dirt. I was suffocating, feeling every jagged, throbbing pain, but I knew I couldn't die down here. Roots were crawling around me now, attaching to my skin and sapping my blood. A root pushed through the ground and pierced right into my chest and stomach, branching out and growing into my body's systems and pathways. Below me, I could feel something pulsing and beating—that same life energy. There was another world below the surface, and I could sense it was filled with things that pushed the boundaries of what a human mind could comprehend. And it was pulling me inward, hungry, wanting to assimilate my energy as a part of it. I was being slowly eaten by Unreal City.

At that moment, my panic and agony and frustration reached a screaming crescendo and power swelled within my chest. With a mighty push, I reached deep within the well of my own thoughts and found a memory of quiet. This world was mine. I was in control. If it was swallowing me and trying to ingest my essence, it was a monster within me that was trying to accomplish this. If I had created that monster, however subconsciously, I still retained mastery over it. With mighty force I pulled my hand away from its pathetic reach for the surface, cut through the earth as if it were mere gel, and grabbed onto my necklace.

As soon as my fingers touched the metal, I felt a bolt of electricity shoot through my body. The darkness that surrounded me shattered like glass. A light brighter than anything that should be perceived by human eyes blew past me — as if it were energy from the source of Unreal City: the luminescence of pure creation. It disintegrated the soil inside of me, burning away the roots as I became flooded by its rushing force. My awareness melted away into oblivion.

11

I AWOKE IN my bed, my chest heaving and my body drenched in sweat. A harried glance out the window told me it was a little past dawn. I mopped my brow with the back of my hand and saw Felix staring at me from the corner of the room. His trademark grin, however, was still not present.

"You —" I gasped, heavy with the memories of being packed into the ground of Unreal City. "You left me there. How could you leave me?"

"I never left you, Sarah," he said, his voice little more than a whisper. "You sent me away."

I didn't have the energy to argue with him. I dragged myself out of bed and down the bunk ladder. The screen of my laptop glowed with a slideshow of photos, many of them containing Lea. I closed the lid, the sight bringing back vivid memories of her flesh rotting away before my eyes.

I didn't have time to process what had happened up there — *down there? Over there? Where is the City?* — before the ringing in my ears began once more, so shrill I collapsed on the bottom bunk, clutching my head in agony. The ringing persisted.

"Felix, what's happening to me? What happened in my garden?" I begged, not strong enough despite my discomfort to get up from the bed that Lea would never sleep in.

"Right now your brain is adjusting to the new way that you experience reality. It will start to pick up aberrations on this side of things. They are essentially 'bleed-throughs' from realities. You're aware of them now because of your heightened sense of perception. You will see or feel bits of displaced energy that haven't quite been …*processed*," Felix explained with a hint of that sadistic amusement. "They cannot harm you, though. What happened back in your garden was an illustration of what takes place if you let your subconscious grievances or desires take over your mind. They take on a will of their own because you allow them too much license, Sarah."

"That would have been *great* to know beforehand, friend," I sneered.

"You never asked." His smile was cruel. I stared at him, gauging his burning, hungry gaze. He was a parasite, a wicked parasite….

"Go. Go." It was on the tip of my tongue to tell him to leave me alone for the remainder of my life, to let this all be a terrible, beautiful memory and go on with things, but I just *couldn't*. I needed to know more, and the fear that I might encounter more drowned victims without my supernatural partner by my side was considerable. Felix had told me that he could fight...that he could *kill*.

"Yes, Sarah?"

"Go—stay in there for a while. Don't come out until I tell you," I said, pointing to the wardrobe on the other side of the room.

Felix looked somber. "In there, Sarah? Why? Have I misbehaved?"

"Just *go*. I don't want to see you for a while."

"Sarah, you won't let me starve, will you?" he pleaded, his ears going back.

"*Go,*" I commanded with a still pointed finger and Felix slinked across the room, opened the wardrobe with his paw, shot me a final look of malicious distaste, and shut himself inside.

I needed to figure out what I was going to do. I sat down at the desk, noticing I had a text from Joy. She had heard about my episode at the crime scene from a friend of hers in the crowd and wanted to know if I was okay. We sent a few texts back and forth, and in an hour's time I found myself sitting on the old, rusty playground carousel, talking with her.

We spun and talked about trivial things—the painted words *seek your bliss* flashing by—and decided a trip to the beach was in order. She was stressed with our project due next week and midterms already around the corner. I found it hard to share her feelings of anxiety over these now-trivial matters, but I sympathized nonetheless. We took a Zip Car down to the city and walked along the boardwalk while sipping smoothies. I brought my camera along, capturing moments here and there—capturing Joy's image and along with it proof that we had known each other. Just in case.

It grounded me to be in this peaceful setting with her. Her good mood never seemed to fade. Once we reached the boardwalk we headed down to sit in the sand.

"So, what *did* happen?" she broached at last.

My eyes were fixed on the churning line of the ocean horizon. The water was silver, as were the clouds veiling the sky, which peeked through in smoky yellow patches.

"I don't know. A boy was killed. He drowned, and I saw his body. It was how Lea died. I just—*lost* it, I guess," I mumbled. I picked up a stick lying nearby and dug around in the sand. The beach was filthy compared to the ones in Unreal City. "I'm just feeling weird lately. I miss my sister.

I'm scared of what might happen—if there's other people dying like her—"

"I can definitely see why," Joy mused, sounding as if she really did understand. "A few of my friends knew the boy that was killed. His name was Tyler Ferguson. The whole school is shocked and horrified, and the police are definitely looking into it." Joy hesitated a moment, then gently put her hand over mine. I shivered under her touch, but it was still nice. "If it is the same person that—that took your sister's life, they're bound to find him, Sarah. They're going to bring him to justice."

"I hope so. I have a weird feeling about all this," I confessed. "I just wish I would've spent more time with Lea before she died. Maybe then I'd know a little more about what happened. Right after she graduated, she spent almost every waking moment with her boyfriend, Stephen. We hardly saw her, and I can't help but feel that there was something she wasn't telling me."

Joy remained silent and let the melancholy moment pass, then scooped up a mound of sand and began building a misshapen castle. After watching her for a moment, I decided to join in.

Our work ethic was impressive. We decorated it with little shells and by the time the sun had sunken away and drenched us in the gloom of night, our kingdom was complete. We talked about past relationships, various friendships that had gone wrong and right, and all the girls that irked us most in our separate high school adventures. Joy joked that nothing really cements a friendship like hating the same things, as dismal as that sounds, and I couldn't help but agree. On our way back, we walked along the shoreline and dug into the sand to find little glowing creatures nestled below the surface. I found them beautiful, but the thought of them buried and packed under the ground like I had been sent a chill running down my spine.

We took the rented car back to campus, making plans to hang out again soon. As I made the journey to the bus stop along a long road lined with wispy, cat-tailed plants, I thought of Felix trapped in the wardrobe.

I should have expected what happened next, given Felix's warning, but it surprised me nonetheless. As I walked along the misty, dim trail, I saw the ground suddenly full of holes. Instead of empty, dark tunnels, they were filled with a pus-like substance, somewhere between mold and swamp water. I could blink or rub my eyes and they would be gone, but then they would gradually return. I tried without success to will them away, and even attempted to run past, but my foot got stuck in the sludge. I wrenched it free and scurried my way to the bus stop, keeping my eyes shut for long stretches of time and forcing my mind to focus on school.

I hurried onto the bus and took a seat in the back. It wasn't long before the bleed-throughs began again. This time it was as if I could hear all the thoughts of the people on the bus. They were echoing off the metallic ceiling, getting louder and louder with every reverberation. I heard worries about money, love, and exams. I heard replayed memories and felt the dismal resonance of someone dreaming of a life they could never have. I covered my ears, but it didn't help. It was inside my head.

The only thing I could do after that was run to my dorm room and leap into bed with the hope of falling asleep quickly. I was wrong. The silence hummed too loudly. My heart would not relent from its quickened tempo.

Hours went by without rest, my body taut, anticipating some horror to visit me in the darkness. My exhaustion, both mental and physical, tormented me. At some point, I think I fell asleep, though I'm not sure. If I had been sleeping, then I dreamt of a human shape with antlers standing outside my window, waiting for me. If I had been awake, then it really was there.

I rose in the morning, my limbs shaking and my head swimming. I crawled down from my bunk and went to the wardrobe to grab a hoodie, screaming when I saw Felix sitting in there.

"Good morning, Sarah. May I come out now? Have you got something for me?"

"N-no. Not right now. Stay in there," I said, shutting him back inside the dark of the closet. I deliberated for a moment, wondering what I was doing by keeping him trapped in there, but chose to turn away.

The week that followed was one of the worst of my life. I tried to get to class as much as I could, but the bleed-throughs plagued me and no matter how I tried I couldn't sleep. On Wednesday morning as I sat in a lecture, the roar of a lion exploded out from the walls. I covered my head and shrieked, and soon realized I had stunned the whole class. I bolted from the classroom, ignoring the stares and questions from the teacher and students. Mortified, I snarled, *"What the fuck are you looking at?"* to two girls shamelessly gaping my way.

I DIDN'T GO to class after that day. I stayed trapped in my room or wandered without direction around the campus. Voices—snippets of pointless conversations from years ago, perhaps, were trapped in certain places and repeated like broken records. Occasionally, my vision would warp, like the world was melting or shifting, and I couldn't do anything but ride it out.

The third night after I'd locked Felix away, I saw the antler-man again. He stalked up to my window sometime after two in the morning. I sat upright in bed and clung to the covers, and Felix began to mewl from inside the wardrobe.

"Felix what's there? What's out there?" I whispered, unable to remove my eyes from the outline of the visitor.

"I don't know! It feels awful though. Sarah, let me out. *Sarah, please,*" Felix whined, scratching at the sides of the wood.

I climbed slowly down from the top bunk, my body shaking as I watched the antler-man watching me. Though his shape was human, with long, shaggy hair, he was too thin, too stretched, his limbs too long. I didn't want to get closer to the window, but I'd have to if I wanted to let Felix out.

"Felix, I can't," I whispered. "I'm scared, Felix."

His meows grew to a screeching, primal wail, and the scratching became frantic. The antler-man took a few steps backward and I thought he would go away, but he stopped and looked over his shoulder toward the window again.

Come back. Come find me. Come back to Unreal City.

The words echoed in my head in a voice that sounded as if it had been spoken by a pair of wet, dripping lips. I shrieked. Felix had gone quiet. A few moments of acute terror passed by and then the antler-man left.

My courage returned too late, and I rushed to the window, needing to know what he looked like. But it was too late—whatever he was, he'd evaporated like mist.

I went to the wardrobe and opened the doors a crack. The inside had been shredded, and Felix's hackles were raised, his eyes wild.

"Did you hear what it said to me?" I whispered to the familiar.

"No," Felix growled.

"If I let you out, what will you do?"

"Feed me."

"Will you run away?" I pressed and Felix bared his pearly teeth.

"*Feed me,*" he insisted, wrath simmering in his voice. I was so frustrated that I ripped out some strands of my hair and tossed them to him. My scalp stung as he gobbled them down like spaghetti, then looked up at me with brighter eyes. "More."

"No, not right now," I told him, then shut the door again. I wandered around the room, anxiety clenching within my chest. I paced until my legs grew shaky and my head dizzy, then collapsed in front of the window. I waited there all night. I was too scared to get back into bed. Too scared to do anything but watch for *him* again. My ears rang periodically with bleed-throughs, and by the time the sun came up, I was hardly conscious. I think I fell asleep on the carpet a few hours after dawn, but it was a restless sleep and my dreams seemed too close to reality to be sure.

The next few days passed as if in a dream, and the only thing that brought me out of my daze was a call from Joy that came late one night—I couldn't be sure how long it had been since I'd seen her. The shock of my phone's ringtone sent my heart pumping madly, but I answered it.

"Sarah, you didn't come to class tonight," Joy said, sounding both annoyed and concerned.

The realization that I'd completely blown off our project hit me like a stone in the bottom of my stomach.

"Oh, my God, Joy, I'm—I'm *so sorry*—" I gasped, my hand to my forehead and my chest tightening with guilt. "I can't even—I have no excuse, I just—"

"Sarah, are you okay? You sound—"

"No," my voice quivered, and I gripped the side of my desk as I put my head down.

"Can I come over?" she asked, and though my pride told me to reject her offer, the mixture of sleep deprivation, prolonged endurance of fear, and isolation had made me weak.

"Please. Please come over, Joy," I begged, my voice warbling. Joy went silent for a moment, and I heard her phone shift.

"I'll be right there. Let me into the dorm when I get there," she said before she hung up.

I waited for her with my head buzzing. For ten minutes I watched my phone's clock, then I put my head down on the desk. Ten more minutes passed.

Where is she?

The ringing in my ears exploded and I cowered, covering my ears with my hands and screaming. My head rolled back as the effort of trying to keep myself together finally snapped. I was unable to even hear my own screams against the ringing in my ears, but the feeling of making such a sound eased some of my angst. As I looked up at the lights on the ceiling, though, suddenly it was like shards of razor blades were piercing my eyes. I toppled backward, covering them, and scrambled blindly to the wall to turn off the switch. I had to stop the pain.

I fell onto Lea's bed, my head throbbing with the echoes of pain assaulting me. Even in the almost complete darkness, it felt like I was staring at a bright cluster of fluorescent bulbs. I crawled under the covers and pulled them over my head, aching for somewhere darker to hide. I stayed there like a caterpillar squirming in the protective shell of its cocoon, until the ringing faded and I realized someone was pounding at my door.

It's him, a terrorized part of my brain whispered. *It's the man with antlers. Don't let him in.*

I quieted this voice and got up from the bed on unsure legs. My hand lay on the doorknob for a while, feeling the knocks pounding on the other side of it.

"Sarah!" Joy's voice came from the other side, and I undid the lock and ripped open the door to see her standing there with a pale face and wide eyes. The stream of light from the hall made my eyes sting, but whatever had happened to make that symptom occur was already fading. The light hurt less now.

Joy looked me over, her expression horrified. "What happened to you?! You wouldn't let me in! I had to wait until other people came along."

I wanted to tell her so badly, but I couldn't. I knew she'd think I was insane—

You are insane.

I burst into tears and started to double over, but felt her hand on my back. Without losing her calm, Joy led me over to Lea's bed. I lay down with trembling limbs until the brief spout of tears ebbed away and my breathing began to stabilize. Joy took a water bottle out of her purse and handed it to me. I drank from it greedily, feeling the water dribble down my chin. It was only then I realized I couldn't remember the last time I'd had a drink of water or eaten.

"Tell me what's going on, please. The other kids in the hall said you were screaming. You look like you need a doctor," Joy said gently.

"No, please. No doctors. I'm fine. I'm just—things are hard right now. Please. No doctors," I begged.

"I can't just sit here while you're sick and not call a doctor. You know that, right?" Joy argued, and for the first time since I'd met her I saw anger cross her face.

I took another long drink of water. "I'm not sick, I promise. I'm just…emotionally overdrawn. I haven't been able to get to sleep, that's why I look like this," I explained, but she wasn't convinced.

"I'm not leaving here until I'm sure you're okay or you've agreed to come with me to the Health Center. You understand that?"

I sighed, but inwardly, I was glad. I wanted someone to stay by my side. I wanted something to comfort me through the storms that would no doubt come again soon.

With Joy around, I was soon steadied and grew drowsy. I lay down and as I started to toss and turn in a state of half-sleep, I felt her fingers touch my neck. My eyes snapped open and I grabbed her wrist.

"I'm sorry, I thought you fell asleep! Your necklace was getting all tangled up around your neck, and I was afraid you might choke, so I was just trying to take it off," she explained, removing her wrist from my grasp.

"I'm sorry, I didn't know what you were doing," I stammered as I straightened my necklace. "I never take this off, though." I held onto the little heart with a firm grip, disturbed at how easily Joy might've separated it from me.

Joy looked down at it. "Is it special to you?" she asked and I nodded, considering my next words.

"It's all I have left of her. They scattered the rest," I said under my breath. It took her a moment to understand.

"Your sister's ashes are inside there?" she guessed, and I turned my head away before nodding. I imagined Joy making a disgusted or scandalized face. I felt strange about it myself, but I couldn't bear to let all of Lea go. I wanted to keep her near to me, always. I didn't expect anyone else to understand this, but I didn't really care what they thought at this point.

"I see. I might've done the same, if I'd had the chance," was all Joy said, nothing scathing or disgusted in her tone, though I almost wished there was. I felt like she should've hated me, left me by myself, or been angry with me. I'd only ever been a poor friend to her; there was no reason for her to be so liberal with her kindness, but it seemed to come naturally to Joy to be endlessly tolerant. She gave freely of her affection and expected nothing in return. I thought I might start to cry again.

"Thank you, Joy. For staying. For everything," I croaked, wanting to tell her more. "I just...I had no idea how much a part of me she was. It's so easy to take people for granted when you think you'll always have them. And it's so much harder when you realize that you'll never get to tell them how much they meant to you until they're already gone." This life had become such a nightmare. I wanted to go back to the time when I didn't have any concept that a human heart could ever feel this much pain. Escaping back into the blissful dreams of Unreal City seemed like the only spot of light in my future now, but even that had been poisoned by the realization that by going there, I was in danger of getting destroyed by my own psyche.

"Tell me more about her," Joy encouraged, and took a seat at the bedside.

In a dreamy, murmuring voice often broken by tremors of grief, I found myself relaying memories of my sister to Joy. How we'd grown up, the games we used to play at the seaside, the trips we went on together, and the silly things we fought about. I told her about how Lea was always looking out for people that needed a friend, and how much of a love-struck teenage girl she'd been. I told her how the summer before she died, she spent almost every day going out to have adventures with Stephen.

Joy seemed interested and shared stories with me, too. She told me about her elementary school days. She'd liked a type of crunchy sugar-crystal candy dyed with bright colors called *Konpeito* that her aunt and uncle would give her every day after she finished her homework. Joy liked antique stores, old things and preserved things. She was captivated by anything retro, nostalgic, forgotten, or obscure. She told me how as a child she'd loved to listen to the Enka and Jazz vinyl records her aunt collected, and how she'd try to draw pictures of the singers' faces the way she imagined them. Listening to her was soothing, and I soon dozed off, caught up musing about her inner world of dusty, precious things.

At some point during my shallow slumber, I felt her climb into the bed beside me and with her warmth there, I was able to sleep the way I used to—deeply and without interruption from the capricious force of dreams. We woke up when light streamed in through the window, and feeling much better I agreed to go get breakfast. After a huge meal and shower, my mood had greatly improved. Joy and I parted ways, agreeing that on Saturday we would go together to the city and get Halloween costumes. She and Kyle had plans to drive down to another university in central California. The town outside that college always threw a raucous Halloween celebration and the rowdy youth came from everywhere to join in the revelry. This didn't seem like my kind of party, or Joy's even, but she was so insistent that I join her I couldn't refuse. I didn't feel like facing Halloween night alone in my room with Felix, anyway.

As soon as Joy left me, the bleed-throughs came back. Back in my dorm, looking at the corner that Felix often stared at, I could feel a force stuck there. There was something trapped in the wall that wanted to leave, but couldn't. I slumped downward with my face in my hands.

"What have I done to myself?" I shuddered. This was going to be my life now. It would never stop, unless…unless I bid Felix leave me forever. I got up, my knees feeling like they might buckle at any moment, and opened the wardrobe doors wide. A weary Felix was sitting on his haunches. "You can come out now."

He silently padded down from his prison, bringing a few curls of wood with him. I knew what he wanted before he even had to ask. I lifted my fingers to my mouth and bit off the tip of one of my nails. Reluctantly I offered it to him, and he licked it right off my fingertip with his sandpaper tongue. Felix looked so bedraggled and abused that I methodically did the same with each finger until he seemed a bit more alive. I had intended to tell him to go away, but seeing him so meek and grateful for what I'd given him, I didn't think I had it in me just yet.

"Felix, come here," I said, patting my legs. He leapt onto my lap and curled his tail around himself.

"The other night, when that force came here. That—
thing—" I began, stroking his spine, "it told me to come back to
Unreal City. What is it, Felix? What does it want?"

"It felt like another familiar, but I couldn't tell who. Its
energy had been warped—twisted. It's like something I've
known forever, but it's been altered. It might have been diseased
with insanity," Felix told me. "That happened often before,
many years ago. Back when mankind was much cruder."

"Why did it want me to come back? If it is a familiar, could
it be the one that killed that boy…and Lea? *Could it have killed
Lea?*" I said it for the first time, though I'd been thinking it for a
while. I had no idea how Lea or the other boy could have been
involved with Unreal City, but I couldn't rule out the possibility. Lea had been so wrapped up with her social life in the
months before she died, I'd never had time to notice whether
or not strange things had been happening around her.

"It's possible. If one of the Cunning Folk had ordered their
familiar to do it, it might've happened…or if they ordered it
to find you in this world, it could also happen. The best you
can do is talk to the person whom you suspect to be at fault,"
Felix told me.

The person whom I suspected was obvious. Angus and
Arthur had both mentioned him: the man they called Poe.
Perhaps if I could only gather the willpower to go and con-
front him, this all might be solved. But for now I was tired—I
was weak. I'd have to hold off from trying to walk unscathed
through the kingdom of a madman until I felt I could safely set
foot in my own garden.

"Don't go, Felix. Don't go just yet."

"I'm yours, Sarah," he purred, shutting his lamp-like eyes.
"I'm not going anywhere."

THE STREETS OF Santa Cruz were fervid with that
special feeling of excitement that only comes the week before
Halloween. Grinning skulls leered from every shop front, fake
purple bats twisted and swung in the wind, and cottony spider
webs adorned the walls of every boutique. The air was crisp
and the damp, smoky scent of autumn floated into our noses
with every blast of wind.

Joy and I meandered through the chattering crowd, our
hair thoroughly fluffed by the October gales. Things didn't
seem so dismal in the daytime, especially when I was with
her. We passed a shop and I caught a glimpse of myself in the
reflection of the window. Large bags had formed under my
eyes and I'd lost at least ten pounds since I got to college. It
startled me. I looked too much like the artificial Lea that had
wasted away before she was reduced to mere bones.

"Here we are!" Joy pulled open the door to one of the Halloween stores that sprung up like weeds before the holiday and
were swept away express in order to prepare for Christmas two
months early. Blinking lights embedded in the heads of plastic

ghouls greeted us as we entered, as did the electronic cackle of some unseen toy. "I'm still not sure which form of 'sexy such-and-such' I'd like to be this year. Let's see what they've got left," Joy said.

She led me through aisles stuffed with decorations, party supplies, and faux weapons. When we reached the row of ladies' costumes, we set ourselves to digging through the disorganized heaps.

"Skanky cop, slutty kitty, risqué pirate wench..." Joy said with an air of boredom as she moved each costume aside. "Oh boy, here's a new one: sexy *Big Bird*. There's something I didn't need to see. What are you thinking, Sarah?"

"Hmmm..." I ran my fingers over the options, not really wanting to walk around in any of them. At the end of the aisle, I saw a fallen hat with a pointy tip.

Of course, I thought as I pulled it off the floor, gave it a quick swat, and placed it atop my head. *I feel almost obligated at this point.* I turned to face Joy.

"I think I'll go with the ol' failsafe this time around," I said. At that moment I began to own the circumstances that had come into my life with a bit of wry humor.

"Somehow that looks really good on you," Joy agreed.

Please don't say that, I thought as I went to pick out a costume to match the hat. Joy settled on a nurse's outfit and we left the store, abuzz with plans for our Halloween night. Back in Joy's dorm we tried on the costumes, and modeling our new personas, I found I liked the way the cheap witch's garb looked on me. It gave me a weird feeling of warranted pride.

While Joy sketched figures at her desk, I lay on the floor, catching up on Sociology. If I did well enough on the midterm I might still pass the class, in spite of my zero on the project. As I tried to focus on the textbooks, I felt a wave of guilt hit me again.

"Joy," I began quietly, setting down my pencil down. "I never really got to apologize for the project. I didn't mean to hang you out to dry like that."

"Please stop beating yourself up over that," she said without looking up from her sketch. "My grade wasn't affected, anyway, so don't get all gloomy over it." She smiled, squinting at the paper.

"I know, but I hate the idea of you just standing up there alone," I admitted. "It's been bugging me."

"You're fine, Sarah. It's not like you blew me off. You were — having a really bad day," Joy said delicately. Her indomitable kindness made me furious on her behalf. I wanted her to value her time, effort, and love more. I wanted her to see how rare it was in this world full of uncaring, selfish people.

"I don't deserve to have you giving me so many chances and so much of your time," I grumbled to myself, still ashamed of my poor contribution to our friendship.

"Please. Enough with the pity party. I like hanging out with you. You're interesting. You sort of inspire me, too, with your strength. You're not afraid to show what's really inside of you, even if the world won't like it. I want to be that — I want to capture that feeling. It's like when I have a picture in my head, and I think how great it'll look on the paper, but when I actually draw it it's nothing like what I imagined. It lacks that sort of raw energy. You do that *effortlessly*," Joy said, still focusing on her drawings, but I felt now it was more to avoid my gaze.

"Well, I'm glad to have you around," I responded.

"Young people often forget, too, that our number of opportunities is limited. True friends come few and far between, and I see so often how people just abandon one another — throw others who love them away so easily because there's something about them that they don't like. What they don't understand is that if you keep cutting out every imperfection, you're not just going to be alone, you're going to be out of chances. Our time isn't as infinite as our age makes it seem, so that's why I want to treasure every person that comes my way, thorns and all," Joy finished with complete candidness.

The rest of the evening passed without even a hint of a bleed-through. I was starting to realize that when my mental state worsened, it was more likely for them to occur. Being near Joy's indestructible good mood was like a panacea.

When it came time to leave, I felt a bit nervous about crossing the campus by myself in the dark, but the costume bouncing in the bag at my side kept my spirits lifted. I found myself thinking that I might be able to get this thing under control, that if I learned to understand and ignore the bleed-throughs, I might be able to stay safe within my own garden. I could make that section of Unreal City mine for the rest of my life. I could even face Charles Poe and demand the answers that I needed to hear, then return all that much stronger. I could do anything I set my mind to.

As I crossed the dizzyingly high bridge over the chasms bursting with their forest overgrowth, I was filled with this new confidence. With my eyes fixed on the pale light of the stars and the crescent moon, I allowed this courage to course through me. Being one of the Cunning Folk was an enormous gift, albeit a ponderous one. So what if I had to give Felix my blood, and let him leech off me for the rest of my time? He'd be my terrifyingly adorable pet vampire. So what if things got weird sometimes? It would never be as bad as it already had been, because I'd grow accustomed to it. And if I lived through getting swallowed by the ground, I could live through anything. If I lived through *losing Lea*, maybe the worst really *had* already passed, and—

Something was standing under the trees at the end of the bridge. Something tall, emaciated, and dappled by the shadows of the pines. I stumbled back, stopping halfway across the bridge to wait and see if I could get a better glimpse. Night gave it the advantage of staying obscured if it wanted to be.

"Hello?" I called, clutching my satchel's strap until my knuckles were white. I could just make out something slipping into the trees. I held my place halfway across the bridge. I didn't want to cross if it was waiting for me, but I didn't think I knew the way home if I went backward. After all was quiet for almost five minutes, I decided to creep forward and see if the way was clear. I kept my eyes fixed on the point in the trees where it had disappeared.

What if it's Antler-Man? What if he decides to kill me? Is he the one who drowns people? I don't want to see what he looks like anymore. Please just let me get home. I wish Felix were here.

Thoughts fired off like the bangs of fireworks in my head. My footsteps made the wood creak. I knew he could hear me coming, if it was him. However, the closer I got to the thicket that he'd slipped into, the more it seemed that perhaps my eyes had been playing tricks on me. It could have been just another bleed-through, a lonely specter, a loose piece of some memory that had been misplaced here in the woods. My shoulders started to relax after I'd made it across the bridge. Just to be safe, I stepped closer to the patch of trees, checking to see if they looked disturbed. Nothing seemed out of the ordinary, so I decided I was in the clear for now. Just as I resumed my walk, a shape as tall and thin as a tree blocked the view of the crescent moon.

I stood trembling in his shadow, resisting the urge to drop to my knees. If I got away, I would never sleep again knowing such a thing existed in this world.

It was a familiar; that much I knew at once. His body was made out of that same solid, ghost-material that Felix's was, but this Spirit's energy seemed *corrupted*. It was the only way I could describe the energy field humming off him. He was at least nine feet tall and his spindly, bony arms ended in hands that looked like tree branches. One arm curled around a vat that he lugged under his skeletal shoulder. Yet it wasn't even the disproportionate body or limbs, or the twisted bones under the wet skin that sent me into a state of such sublime terror. It was his face, his jawless face with its gaping hole of a mouth that dripped gelatinous, watery saliva down his front. It was the image of those chasm-like eyes with their pinholes of light— that same unearthly light that was in all the spirits, the light that burned, made one's head ache, and one's stomach seize up— and that loose, rolling skin under his damp, long hair. That was the image that was seared into my eyes. It haunts me even now. He moved his head, shaggy hair and antlers swinging as a flow of water spewed from his mouth. He lurched toward me as I tried to suck in enough breath to scream.

Unreal City…come back to Unreal City, the spirit's voice boomed. It was coming out of that vat. *I need you. Come find me in Unreal City.*

"G-get away!" I shrieked, trying to keep my head. I knew that if I fell, even for a second, it would be over. If I bolted back, however, I'd be in danger of tripping over the edge into the ravine. So I proceeded slowly, one trembling step at a time as I snuck glances back and prepared to bolt when I had a clear path. The familiar moaned, a low, tortured sound as he shuddered. It was like he had no clear direction of what to do, but was acting under some powerful, emotional influence. More water spewed forth from his mouth-hole, and he lifted the vat upward.

I was just getting ready to make a break for it when I saw the inside of that vat. His voice was in there—and others' too, but they were whispering too quietly to be understood. The reflection of water swirled against the curved sides of the vat, and the longer I looked, the more hypnotized I became. The ripples mesmerized me and the urge to escape waned. Suddenly I realized water was rushing *out* of my mouth, choking me, originating at the back of my throat.

I spat into the dirt and gasped. Just as I felt my throat clear, another gush followed and I was choking all over again, trying my best not fall over.

This is how Lea died. This is how she felt, I realized. With great effort I tore my eyes from the vat, turned, and ran in any direction I could, my feet slipping on the loose dirt. The Antler-Man was howling behind me as I escaped, begging me not to go. More water burst from the back of my throat and tried to rush downward, and I tried swallowing it this time. Most of it went to my stomach, but I was still spluttering and trying to get even one breath of air as I forced my legs to keep going.

I wasn't far from Merrill now. I could make it if I kept going. A smaller rush of water came, and this time I easily spat it out and kept running. I thanked myself for all those extra days I spent at the tennis court back in high school. Skinny as I had become, my legs could still run. By the time I burst through the doors into my dorm, I realized my entire front was covered with water and spittle. What I wanted more than anything was to leap into the shower, but I was too afraid. I needed Felix beside me.

I found my familiar in my room, causally walking around on the ceiling. Catching sight of me, he swooped downward and came to a graceful landing at my feet.

"Sarah, what happened to you?"

"I found him—I found what killed my sister," I gasped, wiping my face on the comforter and pulling my hair back from my forehead. "It was a familiar. Though he didn't feel like how you or the others feel when I get near them. It was like he wasn't in control of himself—just confused. Angry and... and deeply sad."

"What did he do when he saw you?" Felix asked, growing solemn.

"He tried to kill me. Drown me, like he drowned Lea, that boy from my high school, and the kid from here. He's looking for me, I think. He wants me to come back to Unreal City." I was shaking now, and chilled to the bone. I climbed the ladder on shaky legs and crawled into bed. It somehow felt safer there, like the blankets could somehow protect me from even an unearthly being. "What am I going to do, Felix? I can't get help from the police. They'll think I'm insane. I can't tell Joy. I can't even tell my parents how their daughter died. I'm stuck."

"I know what you can do. You can do just what he says."

"*Go back!?*" I was scandalized by the thought. "But that's just playing into his hands! It's obviously some kind of trap, though I don't know what he wants from me."

"Exactly," Felix continued. "But if you don't go and uproot the cause of this problem, it will only continue to grow. Nothing gets solved by simply ignoring it and hoping that it will just disappear. And no one can fix it for you."

"But it's dangerous. I could lose my mind or lose control again," I mumbled in a pointless argument.

"Or you could hide in here forever, fearing for your life while it waits outside your window," Felix said, flipping over his paw in an uncannily human gesture.

"But—"

"Others might be harmed, too. What about that friend of yours, Sarah? Would you endanger her too? Would you want her to meet the same fate as Lea?" Felix's voice was meek, but it was enough to stir me. No. No, I couldn't put Joy in danger. Not Joy, who had been so kind when things had grown so bleak. She was near to me, too. If the familiar was stalking me, then he could easily get to her. I couldn't bear the thought of anything happening to Joy—I couldn't lose another person I cared about.

"And you think this Poe guy will know what to do? You think it might even be *his* familiar?" I tested the waters.

"It's a strong possibility. I don't think Arthur was lying to you."

I sat up in my bed, looking at both of my hands as I considered what choice to make. I thought it over for several long moments, then reached my decision.

"You're right. We've got to find out what he wants. I can't just stay here. I won't let this become my prison. But if I make you promise me something, then you *have* to do it, right?" I asked, feeling quite grave.

"If you make a pact with me, I must obey your every command by the laws of my being. For now, if you give me a gift of food, I shall have to follow your commands for a short while. You'll have more than enough time if you issue them now," Felix told me, and I took a deep breath. Once I said it, there was no going back.

"If I'm about to lose my mind there, in Unreal City — if you know for sure that there will be no hope for me, I want you to promise me that you'll kill me. You'll kill me here in this world."

Felix smiled. "I promise."

13

THE SCISSORS CLIPPED and another lock of my hair came loose. I offered it to Felix, who ate it off my hand with gusto. It must've tasted like a steak dinner to him.

My familiar ordered me to wait, then leapt out the open window. I shut it after he left, frightened that something else might get in during his absence, and opened it again when I heard his claws scratching with squeaks against the glass. He'd returned with that pretty little box that always seemed to disappear by the time I awoke from the fantastical dream. I opened it with caution, and instantly that irresistible smell and the memory of the ambrosial taste hit me. I plucked the petit four from the box and took a deep breath. This could be the last moments of this life as I knew it. An urge to text Joy a goodbye occurred to me, but I knew I couldn't do that—no matter how much it would comfort me. So instead I sent:

> Joy, you've been such a wonderful friend
> to me. I just wanted to thank you for
> everything you've done.

The text found its home, and a sense of finality rose within me. Bracing myself for what was to come, I turned back to the box and devoured the cake in a single bite. No matter how many times I ate it, it was always like tasting that flavor for the very first time. The wonderful poison covered my tongue, and I lay down on Lea's bed as I chewed, waiting for my spirit to leave this world behind for greener pastures.

The departure was smooth. I was floating up, up, up, following the light burning behind Felix's green eyes like a ship nearing a lighthouse. The period of stillness came and passed, and then I was standing in my garden.

It was overrun with plants now, resembling a northwestern rainforest. The first thing I could see was Lea's skeleton, still engulfed by greenery, humming with the artificial life of my world, just like the redwoods. It was host to many things, a living society of different organisms growing out of rot. Yet as I stood there in my quiet misery and looked at those green, blanketed bones sitting so peacefully in the light-falls cascading from the treetops, I had to admit it was beautiful. I approached her, watching the butterflies flutter around the peaceful scene, unaware of the skull buried under the moss and flowers. I touched my hand to the pillar and held it there, checking for the hum of life in what used to be Lea. It was there, even if it was tiny — like a mouse's heartbeat or the hurried beating of wings.

Before I had reached the threshold to the other gardens, I felt the presence of my neighbor. I headed for the opposite end of the rainforest with its dewy leaves and crawling insects, figuring that before I went into the abyss and perhaps forfeited my life trying to discover the truth, I might as well tell someone I had tried.

As I walked I crafted a little piece of paper with a collection of names and numbers on it, then put it inside my pocket. Checking to see that the astral version of the paper still remained in my pocket, I stepped over the threshold into Angus's garden.

I found Angus lying under the shade of Aodh, who resided within the trunk of a massive tree in the center of a magnificent metropolitan paradise. His blue-flame lanterns grew brighter as Felix and I neared. Angus sat up and opened his eyes, greeting us with a warm grin.

"Miss Sarah, it is always a pleasure," he yawned, stretching. "How did it go with creepy Arthur? Didn't mean to drop out on you like that."

"It was fine," I said with a dismissive wave, wanting to get straight to business. "Listen, Angus, I'd like you to do me a favor. I figured out how my sister died."

"*What?*" Angus sat up and straightened his cap. "Did Arthur work it all out after I left?"

"No, I did. It was a familiar, one from this world. But it's gone…insane or something. It's coming after me and killing people at my school. I think it's got something to do with Poe. That he might be after me for some reason. I think he's sending his familiar to hurt me in the real world, so I'm going to go talk to him."

"Sarah!" Angus yelped, jumping to his feet. "Are you out of your mind?! You'll be torn apart. Poe's a maniac. There's no reason he should want to hurt you. He doesn't even *know* you! You're making an awful mistake!"

"I've already made up my mind and Felix will—will help me if things get too scary. I just want to ask you to—if I don't come back, if I get messed up there—tell my parents how Lea and I died. Even if they think it's crazy, will you just tell them?" I pulled the paper out of my pocket and put it in his hand.

"Sarah, you can't do this. I won't let you. You're going to end up like—"

"My mind is made up, Angus!" I shouted at him and turned to leave. I hoped that if worst did come to worst, he'd have a good enough heart to carry out my request.

"Wait! Sarah, there's something I need to tell you first. Stella said not to say but—"

"I don't care about warnings. I don't care about safety. I don't care about the right thing to do," I seethed, my anger appearing out of nowhere once again. "I'm going to find out why my life was ripped apart, come hell or high fucking water."

"You bleedin' idiot, I'm trying to tell you that—"

I ran. I ran until I pierced into my garden, and then set to erecting a wall around the entire place. No one was getting in now. I looked down at Felix, who also looked a bit melancholy, but the more upset everyone was getting around me, the more my courage was fueled. I was going to roll right up to Poe the madman and take what I wanted from him, guns blazing.

"The fastest way will be to fly, right?" I asked Felix, and to my surprise he shook his furry head.

"Poe is different. You can't just drop in to people's gardens who don't want visitors. Arthur's was open because he encourages others to come by. Poe's sealed his up as much as he can. He's paranoid. You'll have to find a crack in the perimeter. I think there's one somewhere near the bottom of his neighbor's garden, from what I remember."

"We'll walk then. Take me there, Felix," I requested and he bowed his furry head and began to stretch out like one of Dalí's elephants. I hopped on his back as he grew and he used his long, crooked legs to step over the wall and into the next garden. He sprinted across Angus's city, stomped through Stella's swamp, and waded across Ranjit's underwater kingdom. The horned familiar swam around Felix's legs as he navigated the choppy waters. Below the surface, diving bells flickered in the dim light.

We crossed his kingdom without incident and made it into the antique Mexican village garden, where the sky took on a twinkling curtain of stars and colored lanterns glowed in the sudden shade of night. As Felix tiptoed between houses, I saw the lavish village was decorated for a festival. Huge bouquets of flowers, banquets streaming with tantalizing scents, and sculptures of skeletons engaged in the height of revelry lined the streets, but there were no people at this celebration.

I thought we would pass right through, but all of a sudden Felix seemed to miss a step and tripped forward. I was thrown from his back and went tumbling toward the dusty, desert ground. Screaming, I expected the fall to crush me and leave me with a slew of broken bones and a smashed nose, but the ground below me crumbled upon impact. I kept falling, getting buffeted as I smashed my way through caverns against the hard and jagged stones.

At last the terrible fall came to an end and I lay moaning at the bottom of a sandy pit, bleeding, and with the sensation of broken glass filling my arm. I took several gasping breaths and managed to sit up. My ribs felt shattered and I could do little but sit there and gasp as waves of pain assaulted me. The little shaft of moonlight where the ground had broken apart looked miles above me. I was lost amid the darkness of an underground system of caves. A shallow layer of water and sand filled the caverns, but they seemed relatively clean and spacious. It might have been interesting, had I not been bashed to pieces.

With a hoarse voice I called up to the surface, hoping that Felix could hear my cries, but no reply came. I took a deep breath, which felt like nails being driven into my sides, and tried to stand without success. I had failed even before I got to look Poe in the eye. I prayed Felix would fetch me so I could return to my garden and heal.

Rapid footsteps interrupted my thoughts; someone was barreling toward me through the caverns. Within moments a woman with long black hair wheeled around the corner, hyperventilating. It looked as if she meant to run past me, but I shouted to her and she came to an echoing halt.

She clutched her chest with obvious panic. "*¿Quien eres?*" she questioned, pointing at me with a shaking hand. "*¿Qué hace usted aquí?*"

"I…I'm sorry. *Uh, lo siento,*" I stammered, reaching out pathetically and wishing I'd paid more attention in my high school Spanish classes. "*Mi — mi bones. I'm hurt. Por favor, um — ayuda me!*"

She began talking rapidly and pointing backward, but I would not be swayed by her hysterics though her react frightened me. If something was coming I needed to be able to run. I kept pointing to my legs and ribs and screaming, "*Ayuda me.*" I hoped that my memory served me and this meant "help me" like I thought. She realized what I meant and hurried to my side, placed a hand on my legs, and I felt much of the pain ebb away. Although I still ached, I could at last stand again.

"*Apúrate! Corre!*" she said. "*El balsero, el viene!*"

Without another glance in my direction she took off running. I had no idea what she'd said, but she sounded terrified. I stood there a little longer, frightened of what I might see coming down the tunnel after her.

"*Felix!*" I screamed up to the patch of light so far above my head, but still no answer came. In the silence after my echo dissipated I could hear a scuffling sound echoing through the caves. Water sloshed, sand shifted. The sound of something scuttling and clicking on stone grew closer.

I froze, pressing myself against the cavern wall as a set of four eyes, devoid of pupils and glowing with the singeing light of the familiars, loomed out of the shadows. Each was as wide and round as a dinner plate. I gasped as a monstrous crab scuttled into the feeble light. Its body was covered in razor sharp spines and horns, and it had one massive claw it dragged along in the shallow pools, flexing it as if itching to catch something.

Not daring to breathe again, I waited for the massive creature to pass by on its hunt for the poor, tormented woman. Either it had no interest in me, or it hadn't seen me, because it left without as much as a sideways glance. Trying to catch my breath and slow the manic pounding behind my ribs, I crouched down and hugged my knees. I don't know how long I waited there, but I kept my eyes closed until I heard Felix calling to me from the surface. I screamed back. I couldn't navigate this world without him. My wonderful, wonderful cat fluttered down as if riding upon a breeze and landed beside me.

"Sarah, forgive me," he said, rubbing his head against my aching legs. "I lost my step. But we're almost there. I think we can get to Poe's garden through here. Are you in pain? Can you walk?"

"I'm okay. A woman came by and helped me," I told him, getting to my feet and taking a few steps forward, gritting my teeth every time my foot hit the ground.

Felix led me onward through the dark. I staggered and huffed the whole way, hearing my ragged breath bounce off the cave walls. Felix picked up speed, and it felt as if my legs would snap apart again if I kept up with his pace. I came close to begging that we turn around and return to my garden, where I knew I could be safe and free from pain, but I pressed onward, determined to have my answers at last.

At the darkest part of the cave, where almost no light penetrated except the brilliant green of Felix's eyes, we hit the membrane that separated gardens. Except instead of passing through it with a simple step like normal, there was a wall of black rubble blocking the way, covered in a mess of graffiti. I saw letters that looked like a made-up, disorganized form of writing, beside things like "*Toynbee Idea in movie 2001 resurrect dead on planet Jupiter*", "*Kill every cameraman*", and "*Lasciate ogne speranza, voi ch'intrate*". I touched the stones with their strange collage of words, and they felt sharp, but porous, like volcanic rock.

"How do we get through?"

Without answering Felix swatted at the side of the wall with his paw. The force of the impact was unbelievable: most of the rocks blew apart in a shower of dust and bits of stone. Through the hole that he'd created I could see little bits of blackness and rushed forward to move some of the rocks out of the way. Felix assisted me with controlled swats.

A tight, jagged crawl space appeared at last. The idea of entering, however, scared me more than anything else thus far. What if the tunnel led to nothing and I got trapped in there, unable to turn around? What if the other side caved in and I got stuck, crushed by the ground, suffocating and undying like before?

"I'll go first," Felix offered, sensing my aversion. "If we get caught, I can claw us out." Without hesitation, my brave little spirit wormed his way into the hole and I followed, crawling on my hands and knees while my bones screamed in protest.

The sides of the rock cut and poked into me. The air grew stale and full of dust. I coughed so much it hurt to breathe.

"I don't think I can make it," I rasped after only a few minutes. The space was getting too tight and I was getting cut to shreds by the rocks. I couldn't get through, and I couldn't go back.

"No, Sarah. You can't stop halfway through. You have to keep going," Felix insisted. "Your wounds, your pain—they will be impermanent. Endure it."

My face damp from tears and my lips slick with spittle from the coughs likely ripping wounds in my throat, I crawled forward, not caring how pathetic I looked or acted. We weren't even close to the end, not at all. We'd only gone about one-fifth of the way, and it seemed as if I would lose my mind before we reached the place where the tunnel let out. When Felix at last swatted at the end of the wall and blew a hole that sent a wave of fresh air and light flooding toward us, I scrambled out like a wild animal running for its life. I tumbled out of the rock tunnel, assumed the fetal position on the ground and lay there, crying. It only took one tear-clouded look at my hands and arms to tell me that I'd become the human equivalent of Santiago's prized marlin. Felix pawed over to where I lay trembling and licked at my wounds.

I drew away as a spike of panic drilled at my heart. *My blood, did he taste my blood!?*

"The pact cannot be made in the Unreal City, Sarah. It's not your real blood, don't worry," he reassured me, and went back to licking my arms and face.

It somehow made the pain feel less real, and I let him tend to me for a while before I rose to my feet and wiped as much of the blood on my pants and shirt as I could. The worst part was having to pull two flags of loose, torn skin off my arms, but once I left them lying there on the barren, rock-littered ground, I felt a reluctant, yet strong second wind fill my tired body.

We stood in the middle of a dry wasteland. The ground was parched, yet above the sky was pregnant with black, swirling rainclouds. Not a sprinkle of moisture was in the air, but the air shivered with the threat of lightning. The long-dead, dehydrated skeletons of trees dotted the dry expanse, and it seemed as if this arid, parched hell stretched on forever.

"Find him," Felix instructed. "Time's already running out. You don't want to have to go through all of this again, do you?"

"No," I sighed, disheartened at the ugly eternity of desert that stretched out before us.

"Then you should run." Felix took off like a black fish streaming through the ocean and I had little choice but to follow.

I ran until I was sure the memory of this pain would remain in my physical body for months after this nightmare. My lungs stung and my body was drenched with sweat. At least four of my toes felt broken and blisters formed, then split open on my heels. Felix shouted back to me over and over again, urging me to keep hurrying. If I gave up now, it would all be for nothing.

My thoughts became distant and hallucinatory. I was barely conscious, barely understanding where I was, letting my legs propel me forward as I got further and further away from my pain. In the very distance, I thought I could see a little hovel sitting in the center of the wasteland. As we neared it, Felix picked up speed, his eyes wild.

Lightning struck down twice as we grew closer, accompanied by the sound of thunder splitting the air. The hovel was clearer in my sight now, and I saw it was no larger than a simple, one-room shack constructed out of what looked like rotten driftwood. The door hung ajar and swung a little in the stuffy air that filled this world like a miasma. I could feel the presence of one of the Cunning Folk and a familiar inside those poorly constructed walls, yet his was unlike many of the others. It had a flavor of corruption, like a computer's programming that had fallen into disarray but still tried to work, still carrying out the commands even with the inherent flaws that could never be remedied.

When we were within a few feet of the hovel, something bizarre occurred. All of a sudden, it wasn't like we were running forward, but rather *falling* toward the building, though the perspective didn't change—just the feeling of gravity. The expanse lengthened and my scope of vision stretched, along with the feel of my body. The world was flattened, and it sucked both Felix and I into it. I tripped over my own feet, stunned by the strangeness of what was occurring.

Just as suddenly everything snapped back to the way it should be, and Felix and I both sat on the ground, trembling. We were mere feet from the door of the shack, and drew closer to one another as it opened with a creak and revealed a small, dusty room. Trembling, I stood to my feet and peered inside.

14

"HE-HELLO? IS ANYONE in there? I need to talk to you." I craned my neck a little more with each cautious step into the hovel.

The first sight I beheld was of a teapot standing on a rickety old table. However, when I looked at it, all the parts of it seemed disconnected. The spout was floating upward and the handle looked like it was in front of everything else, and I just knew if I touched it that it would feel normal. This peculiar illusion hurt my eyes and I didn't want to look at the thing, but the more I tried to break away, the more I became fixated on it. Something about that teapot and its spinning, moving, impossible parts and the lurid, floral design made me forget about everything else.

It's making me feel sick. It's making me want to puke. It's making me remember the time at the café when I was watching that girl and she didn't know that I knew that she'd been changed, the most sinful change, that she wasn't one of us but I knew about her. I knew that she was watching me from inside that teapot, where they were

talking softly about the game that only the dead security guards knew
how to play and how those orange cigarette burns would –

I kept blinking and shook my head, trying to shake out the thoughts. They dispersed and I gasped for breath, adamantly keeping that infernal object out of my sight. I had felt my mind slipping away, and it scared me – badly. Those mad, winding thoughts would start again if I looked its way, so instead I turned my eyes past the table to the corner of the room where a man sat on the floor.

Skin, much of the muscle tissue, and organs had been eaten away from the front of his torso, leaving a glistening, black-brown ribcage strung with stray fibers of flesh. From inside the ribcage, I could see something crawling around and gnawing its way deeper into the man's core. However, from the neck up, he was still whole. His bald head was glazed in sweat and printed with tattoos that reached over his gaunt cheeks and hollow, haunted eyes. He turned and smiled at me, gesturing lifelessly with his arm.

The crawling thing emerged from under his ribcage, and I saw it was a scorpion with the head of some other animal – perhaps a bear or wolf. Its exoskeleton was a poisonous red, dotted with spots that pulsed with the familiar's light, its eyes unfocused and wild as it scurried up the man's neck to the crown of his head, clicking it claws and gnashing its teeth. The man looked at me with his hazy black eyes and laughed at my apparent revulsion as the flesh on his torso began to regenerate.

Felix was not reckless enough to lead this time, and it was I who took the first step into the low-roofed shack.

"So you've finally come to do away with me."

"D-do away with you?" I stammered.

The man's eyes widened as Felix entered, staying close to my ankles. "No, so, it's not you after all. You're not the one who's following me, are you? You can never be too careful," the man breathed, and then his defenses rose. He stood up, his torso complete again and his chest now covered with the same types of intricate tattoos as his head. The creature atop his head opened its mouth wide and hissed.

"Are you Charles Poe?" I asked, my voice shaking. I balled up my fists, letting the fear-fuelled anger inside of me grow. It wasn't courage, but it was better than nothing.

"Why do you want to know? What have you come here for?" he demanded frantically, and I put up my hands in a gesture of peace.

"Arthur — the man at the library. He told me you were being followed by a familiar, not in this world, but in the other. One that's got antlers on its — "

He sucked in a deep breath through his teeth and the scorpion's claws began clicking madly. The man was trembling as he pointed an accusatory finger in my direction, but I was not about to be chased away.

"*It's after me too!* I need your help. I need to know what it is. It killed my sister."

"There's nothing you can do. Run. Hide. Never tell your name to anyone again. Take the pills your kitty-cat gives you. Take the medication. It'll keep you here. It'll keep you stable," the man advised, shrinking back from me as if I had a contagious plague.

I held fast. "No. I'm not going to let it destroy anyone else's life. Tell me what it is."

Poe gave a shrieking laugh that turned into a bellow of rage. As he did, lightning began to ravage the ground outside and the shift of gravity occurred once more. I fell over, reaching for Felix and catching him. The storm subsided and I stayed on the floor, hugging Felix to my chest.

"It's from Hell. It's a living sin. It's the harbinger of all of our dooms, little bitch. Spoiled brat. So you better fucking run, run, run as fast as you can, little girl," he cried, hysterical laughter interspersed with sobs. "Once it sees you, it'll never stop."

"That thing there. That's your familiar, isn't it?" I breathed as I pointed to the scorpion, realizing I had fallen into this hellish pit only to find another dead end — one that might cost me my sanity and my life. Poe lifted the scorpion down from his head and cradled it in his arms while it tore at the flesh on his wrists.

"*This* is a parasite," he said darkly. "But I need my medication, so I've got to pay my abominable piper. That demon is a parasite, too, but it's lost its master. It needs blood. It needs orders. It's just doing what it was told to do in the moment before its master went away, over and over and over. It's lost."

"Why is it chasing *us*, then?"

"Because its master told it to. He *hated* me. He thought I didn't deserve to live, so he sent it after me to do me in," he sputtered, and the scorpion crawled down the side of its head and began to chew its way into his ear.

"Well, then why did he send it after *me*?" I insisted.

"I don't even know who you are," he said, his eyes rolling backward as the scorpion disappeared into his head, his earhole leaking a stream of blood. "You probably crossed him wrongly, or wrongly crossed him somehow."

"How can I stop it then? Do you know?"

"It won't sleep until it has blood. Until it has a new master. Give it blood." Poe smiled and the scorpion's claws pierced his neck from the inside out as it started to chew its way out again.

"I'm not going to make a pact with that thing!" I yelled in a knee-jerk response, and he shook his head, more blood dripping from the hole in his ear.

"Don't have to. Give it another person's. Have you met my beautiful neighbor, Miss Jezebel?" Poe asked and he pointed in the direction we had come from. I guessed her to be the woman who had been running from the crab, so I nodded.

"She is here because she did a bit of back-stabbery, or so Arthur says. Jezebel stole her sister's man, so her sister calls up that demon in the night and gives her a bit of dear Jezzie's blood, then hides that sugary skull he trades her in her sister's food. When she's here, she's being punished. She has no idea what happens to her, nor will she heed the voice of the parasite," Poe explained to me. "You gotta do the same. Give it blood, and it will go away. It will go away."

"But why can't you do it?" I asked him, sickened at the idea that I'd have to submit another person to this cursed life that I had stumbled into so foolishly.

"Don't know anyone. Won't go out, no one will come in. I'm trapped." Poe sank to the floor and covered his face with his hands as the scorpion began its feed all over again. This man's eyes told the story of his pain and I could feel it saturating me the longer I stayed in his domain. It made my chest ache. The feeling of alienation and heightened nervousness ate away inside of me, just like that scorpion ate at him.

"Look, mister, I'm gonna find a way to stop him. I'm gonna make him leave you alone. I'll help you," I promised him. Beneath my fear of this man, I felt pity for him, like I understood some tortured part of his tired soul, even if it was just a fraction.

His woebegone smile broke my heart. "You can't help me. No one can help me. I was born with poison in my mind."

His last sentence repeated over and over, like it was coming out of a reedy old sound system inside the walls. I locked eyes with Poe as the phrase continued to resonate, growing more indistinct and peculiar to my ears. It started to grate on me, to hurt me like the sound of Styrofoam scraping against itself. I cringed from the sound and intensity of Poe's stare.

"Oh, God, Jesus, Lord and Savior, I remember you. You fucking demon, you self-indulgent little pig, you whore," he cried, his voice suddenly full of malice. The scorpion crawled out of the hole in his neck and perched atop his shoulder, its eyes fixed coldly on me. "I know who you are, you liar, you filth. You're helping him. You came here to give my position away. You came here to help him find me. You prey on the good people. You pretend to be kind, but you're a vulture, a biting spider." He was raving now, shaking from head to toe with rage as the scorpion opened its toothy jaws and hissed at me.

"Run, Sarah," Felix said softly in my ear. I didn't need telling twice. I leapt to my feet and bolted from the room.

Outside, lightning was pulverizing the cracked earth. Glancing back, I could see Felix was behind me, and behind him the scorpion and its master. The gravity shifted four more times as we dashed across Poe's garden. Each time I was on the verge of falling, but I kept on running. I would not fate myself to Poe's mercy.

The gravity shifted again, but this time with it came a new scene. We now stood at the edge of a balcony with nowhere to go but a dizzyingly high drop. Black pine trees stretched upward and in the boughs sat three owls with impossibly large eyes. I stumbled to a halt, paralyzed by these owls that looked so still and threatening. A quick glance backward told me Poe and his familiar were still advancing, thundering down a hallway toward us.

"Jump!" Felix urged, and I trusted him. We leapt off the balcony together, the eyes of the owls following us.

There was no bottom to this fall. Once the tops of the trees left our vision, Felix and I plummeted downward into nothingness, frantically reaching for one another in midair. I grabbed the tip of his tail and pulled him close. Pure terror reigned while I tried to think of any way out of this, which intensified when everything froze. We were suspended in midair for what felt like eons, until out of the gloom I saw something materialize in front of me.

It was an image of myself holding Felix, only reversed. It took me a second to realize I was staring at a mirror that stood between two stone arches, and that ground now lay beneath my feet. I turned, only to see that another mirror blocking the way behind me. I turned again: another mirror.

"This way," Felix said, leaping from my arms and marching forward through what I thought would be glass barring his way. When his reflection didn't run up to block him, I hurried after him. "It's a maze. He knows he can't keep us trapped here. There are always cracks in every person's mind, so he's trying to confuse us. Keep us lost until he can get here first. If we run, we can make it."

Felix and I took off through the mirrored maze. I felt a little wonderstruck by the repeating hallways and pristine glass that bridged the way between the stone arches. I could see dozens of reflections of myself—bruised and bloody—at every angle. It was almost hypnotic, until I heard the hissing, wolf-like cry of the scorpion beast and the thundering footsteps of Poe.

Of course, he made *this maze. He knows how to solve it.*

My heartbeat accelerated a hundredfold; I had to get away. Dead end after dead end barred our way, and the madman's footsteps were growing closer. I felt myself succumb to hysteria.

"Can't you just bust a hole in it?!" I hissed at Felix. He reared back and took a swipe at the wall, but his claws bounced off.

Suddenly, there he was. There, glazed in sweat and bearing his teeth, was Poe. I put up a hand to protect myself, then realized it was only his reflection that I saw. I ran in any direction I could, twice slamming hard into a mirror and seeing his image hounding me wherever I went. Forcing myself to keep going, I pummeled hard into a pinched end and when I turned to go back, I knew it was over. He'd caught me.

Felix stood between the advancing madman and me. Glee was apparent on Poe's face, his lips twitched in a perverse smile, the scorpion scuttling at his bony feet. Felix hissed, baring his fangs.

The scorpion struck first, leaping on Felix and stabbing him viciously with his barbed tail. The two rolled over one another, ripping with claws, tearing with teeth, fierce in their urge to destroy one another. Poe sidestepped the brawl and came toward where I was cornered. A sob escaped my throat, and I sunk to the ground, my hands over my face.

"It's because of you. It's your fault that I'm this way. And because of that I'm going to take you apart and give you the punishment you deserve. You did this to me. You're rotten to your very core," he whispered, reverent, as though reading scripture from a sacred book. "I'm going to take from you what I could never have."

Poe lifted his hand. The sound of the familiars' rage behind him was growing more intense as he snapped his fingers and a bright thread of white light blossomed from his fingers. He brandished it in the air like a whip and brought it snapping down over my shin. It cut like an electric saw through balsawood. Searing pain shot up my leg and my screams reverberated through the mirrored halls. My head thrashed, my eyes bulged, and I could see it happening all too clearly, reflected all around me. I felt every pulse of agony as a rush of blood seeped from my stump of a leg. Poe was laughing at me, empowered by what he'd done. With gusto he reeled backward again and spun that horrid light-whip through the air. I put my arms up to block it, and in a flashing instant of spiraling torture, I saw my left arm drop off and hit the floor. Blood was quickly filling up my little corner and the sound of Poe's laughter was drilling into my ears. Every inch of my being perceived pain.

He knelt beside me, putting his sweating, smelly head close to mine. "You have no idea what kind of a person you are, do you? You deserve this," Poe whispered, his breath warm and wet on my face. He lifted a grungy finger and his nail lit up white-hot like the whip. He grabbed my forehead and pinned my head to the side of the mirror, then took aim. I could see in the reflection that he was going for the soft area between my jaw and ear.

The first puncture felt like a drill bit going into my head. My scream came, gurgled, and tears streamed down my cheeks. I caught sight of Felix scratching madly at the scorpion's shell. Our eyes locked as Poe started to cut along my jawline.

"Help me," I whispered to my familiar.

Without hesitation, Felix leapt over the scorpion to me, his claws extended. Poe drew back in surprise and with a staggering force my spirit slammed him into a mirror. The glass shattered and Felix tore into Poe's chest, ripping off large hunks of his skin with every swipe. I crawled forward and seized a mirror shard that sliced my fingers. I leaned over to Poe and looked him straight in the eye as he tussled with Felix.

"I—am—*innocent*." I plunged the mirror shard deep into his chest, and this time I enjoyed his scream.

Felix held him down as I picked up my fallen limbs from the floor. Out of nowhere, the officious little beast of Poe's stabbed the foot still attached to my body with its stinger. The burn of its poison hit me with the force of a bullet. I clutched my severed arm and leg close to me, holding them in a vice-grip as I convulsed. Felix pushed Poe away, and with one decisive bite, snipped the wolf-like head off the scorpion. Its teeth continued to champ and its eyes rolled as it lay on the floor.

Felix wrapped his tail around me. It stretched out, curling over and over until I was coiled up in his bonds. "Hold on, Sarah," was his only warning before he tossed me and I went shooting up.

I burst through the ceiling in a shower of glass and stone. My body went limp as I sailed through the clouds and starry sky, which looked as if it were the curved inside of a snow globe. Felix had thrown me into the airway above Poe's garden.

Then I fell. I fell holding the pieces of my mangled body and watching my blood and tears stream upward into the air. My eyes shut, my face contorted, and I was swallowed up by the sound of wind roaring in my ears. It was the most nightmarishly sublime moment in my life, not knowing where I was falling to or what would happen when I hit the ground. But a large part of me didn't care anymore. For those few brief seconds when I was falling, I was free.

15

WATER MET ME at the bottom. But it didn't knock the life out of me, or even sting my wounds. It swallowed up my body gently, as if I was sinking into a warm bath instead of being tossed by ocean waves, yet it stretched farther than my eye could see. As I sank deeper, I could see the surface above me. Trails of my blood showed how far I was going, and when I let my head roll to the side and all the air escape from between my lips, I saw that the sun was beside me and not above me. I stared into its burning glory as I went deeper and deeper into this warm ocean. When I came to a gentle rest at the bottom, the sensation of being underwater dissipated, but that massive, flaming sun remained.

Clutching my severed arm and leg, I felt the wetness evaporate from my clothes and rolled my bleeding head around. I was lying on a sandy plateau high, high above a desert. The sun was so huge it filled a great portion of the sky, yet it was sinking below the horizon and its brilliance painted the space behind it with many vibrant colors: pink, orange, yellow, and misty blue. And it was warm. The gentle heat soothed the sting in my wounds and dulled the ache of the hole drilled into my jaw. I drank in the rich colors of the desert many miles below where I lay, then shut my eyes again. Exhaustion had won.

"Child," came the deep rumble of a man's voice, gentle and soft. "What has brought you to such a sorry state?"

"My sister," I whispered, thinking only of my broken heart and not my body. "She's gone. I tried to make it right, but I couldn't. I wasn't strong enough." I felt a tear slip down my cheek. "I'm tired."

"Put yourself back together," the voice ordered.

I wanted to resist it, to lie there in pieces and just bleed into the sand forever, but I could not ignore the command. With titanic effort, I heaved myself up with my one arm and let the two limbs fall from my grasp. I picked up my arm from the ground first and stuck it back where it belonged. The muscle and blood were cold against my wound when I first pressed it to my bleeding stump, but warmth soon flooded into it and it re-attached. A tingling sensation lit up my fingertips, and I wiggled my fingers and smiled numbly at the miracle. Next I put my leg back on, and whole again, I lay back down in the sand. The warmth of that burning sun was miraculous. I actually felt at ease. I took another deep, healing breath, then turned to see who the voice belonged to.

At the edge of the plateau, an old man sat staring at the sun in quiet meditation. His dark hair was braided and his eyes possessed a serene wisdom that I knew I could never fathom for as long as I lived. At his side stood a bull, its head clean of flesh and fur, but its skull painted with the mesmerizing images of the southwestern desert. In the intricate feathers and beads that decorated this creature's head, I saw the luster of deep magic.

I worked up enough strength to crawl over and sit beside this man. For a long while, we fixed our eyes on the majesty of that sun in complete silence.

"What is this place?" I dared to ask as curiosity overcame me.

"The tallest mountain, the center of the world. It is all places and all things. It is the axis," the man said, a cryptic mischievousness in his voice. I thought over what he meant and decided it was best to let such words resonate through me, to swallow them up and digest them and hope that the importance of them would become so assimilated that one day it would all make sense. "Tell me, child, what is it that you are thinking?"

I considered my thoughts for a moment, and they came spilling out in a flood of emotion. "I'm remembering a time before this. Before any of this. I remember a time when there was tenderness in my life, when things didn't seem too harsh and cold and hard. I have a memory of hope, and of excitement, and of promise that my life was just beginning. That it would go to so many wonderful places. Things felt fresh once. Things were simple and smiles came easily — naturally. I remember loving people, coming to know and trust strangers and believing with all my heart that they would never hurt me. Safety was something I took for granted and I thought that she and I would go on forever. I never thought that I would end up like this. I would do anything to have that back."

"And what took this from you?"

"My sister did. Lea took it when she died, and no matter h-how hard I try to hold on, I—I feel like I'm losing more and more. I'm forgetting her. I'm *already forgetting her*. The sound of her voice, and the moments we shared. I'm losing a bit more every day. She's fading from my life, and I can't do anything to stop it." Tears came now, and I clutched my chest and hung my head, feeling powerless against the pain that gripped my battered heart. "I thought I could fix it by finding out what happened to her, but I just—I don't know what I should do anymore."

"You should let her go."

"How can you say such a thing?" I bit back, looking at him with rage, but he would not meet my gaze. "I would rather die than forget my sister."

"I can offer you that, if you'd prefer," he told me. "Stare into that sun long enough and I will make it burn so brightly that your mind will be lifted from you. It will happen gently, easily, like being lulled into the deepest and most wonderful sleep. Everything that you are will fade, and back on the other side, your friend will take your life from you before you even wake. Your pain will cease for all time, and you will be freed from the burden of life."

"How did you know about the promise Felix made?" I whispered.

"I see all things, because it is what I desire most. It is what I create in this realm," he told me calmly, a fatherly smile on his smooth lips. "Now, Sarah, will you let me sing you to sleep? Or will you rise fighting?"

"I—" I was stunned, tempted by the thought of being able to leave this world behind for the sweet, endless sleep where I would be free from pain and turmoil. But I was terrified to disappear—to let go of the soul I had built out of—no, earned from the trials of my life. Thoughts of Felix, who had so bravely fought to save my mind, and perhaps my life, from the ferocity of Poe stopped me. What a shame it would be to see such a good-hearted deed squandered. I thought, too, of Joy. It was on her behalf that I'd returned to this world of exquisite nightmares. This meager attempt, however trying it had been, would not suffice. I had to keep going. But going forward felt impossible at that moment.

"I want to live, but I don't want to live like this," I told the man. "It hurts too much."

"It hurts because you are holding on to your pain. You keep it like an anchor around your shoulders. You won't let it pass. Nothing new can grow in poisoned soil. You befoul it by your own hand; you plant seeds of dead things, and sate their unquenchable thirst with your tears. Let it go."

"But I *can't*. It won't go. It stays with me. She was such a part of my life—so much a part of me. Lea and I were born together. She brought meaning to my life, and assurance, and peace that I can't get from anywhere else. She took my ability to love things and love life when she went. I can't get that back, so all I can do is remember. Without those memories, I'll—I'll be nothing. Nothing at all." I hadn't realized it, but I was crying again, except without the shame and anger it often accompanied. I faced the man with tears shining on my cheeks, but he would not turn from the sun.

"You are wrong again," he told me with grave certainty. "Your sister brought those things out in you, she did not provide them. You celebrated your ability to love on a worthy subject: a soul who helped you recognize all the beauty in the world. It wasn't something she gave to you, or that you lost when she left. It's still within you. It is immeasurably difficult to sow a field of your own dreams, by your own hand—but the yields are more precious than anything you will ever come to know."

"I…I understand, but how can I just accept this? How can I make my heart stop aching? How can I be peaceful in the knowledge that I'll never see her again? That she's gone?" I pressed, because I knew he was right.

My mother used to say that the truth really *rings* when you hear it, but you have to listen for it. She meant that there's a place inside of you that can almost feel the vibration when someone is speaking the truth, and that it flows through you and washes all the doubt away. She said "You'll know it when you feel it" and I'd never had any idea what she was talking about until that moment.

"She's not gone, child. Death is an illusion. She is merely changed. Energy survives. We are, each of us, a raindrop. We fall through the air and are shaken about by winds, but eventually we all come to the ocean. At that point, the droplet is gone, but it has become a part of something bigger and more wonderful—a whole system of energy, changing and living and dying over and over again until time will once again cease. She is not lost, she is everywhere," he said, and at last turned to look at me.

His eyes were startling in that orange light, and the sight of them made my tears come even more violently. I leaned into my hands and sobbed, feeling an ache more powerful than anything I'd known up until then coursing through me. It started at the base of my spine, shot through my neck and out my eyes. The deluge of tears poured, my eyes stinging with the emotions traveling through them. I felt as though little shards of glass were falling from my eyes and pooling in my hands, and the mixture of the pain, fear, and grief just seemed to feed my paroxysm. I cried for what seemed like forever, but the tears stopped when I realized they had frozen together in my hand.

I gazed in shock at a beautiful dagger formed by my tears, radiant as though carved from a single diamond. Its facets reflected the brilliant light of the sunset and when I turned it around to grip it by the hilt, it felt light and natural to my palm.

"What is this?"

"It's yours. You earned it. Use it to defend yourself. Use it to get to the deep place," the man told me. "Now you must go, little Raindrop. Your time here is fading, and a spirit waits for you in your garden."

"Felix!" I gasped. I'd forgotten all about him in my moment of self-pity, but the mention that he'd made it back to the garden brought me to my feet in an instant. I rushed away from the sun, but skidded to a halt just before leaving. I looked back at the man, who'd gone back to his meditation, and opened my mouth to speak.

"Thank you," I said quietly, knowing he'd hear. I almost asked his name, but after thinking about it for a moment, I chose not to. With the diamond-knife in my hand, I rushed away and leapt through the wall of his garden. By the time I passed through another garden, which was a series of endless plains with little villages nestled in the hillocks, I realized I should've taken the airway home.

Thankfully I was approached by the stoic, grizzled man with the Kelpie familiar. We exchanged a hurried greeting and I begged him to send me up to the airway. He complied without another word and I found myself gliding over the City on a gust of wind and down into my garden. As I neared the surface, I felled the walls that I had raised upon my leaving with a wave of my hand. I sped through the greenery that had all but taken over the place, rushing about and calling for Felix.

There was no sign of the familiar or the pillar that encased my sister's bones. A fogginess started to descend upon me, and I knew there wasn't much time left in Unreal City. Desperate now, I screamed for Felix. Had the man lied when he said that he was waiting for me? Was Felix still trapped with Poe?

I heard his little mewl from a few feet away. I hurried forward and found him lying curled up in a clump of ferns. He was covered in wounds, and his bones were exposed in several places. He was licking at his wounds. I knelt beside him, scooped him into my arms and willed him to be healed. The patches of blood and torn flesh repaired themselves.

"Thank you for what you did," I said quietly, the fogginess in my mind becoming oppressive.

"I think I've made the mistake of growing fond of you," he whispered back.

I was tired again, and I lay down in the greenery with Felix in my arms. He rested his head against my shoulder. A light, powdery snow started to fall and soon the whole forest was covered in frost. We were being crystallized, both too weary to mind. Snow kept falling, and as my clarity of mind began to slip, I wished everything would stop. Stop forever, remain frozen here in the snow — though I knew now that this could not be.

In the last moments before the vision of Unreal City faded, I held onto that desire, clinging to the belief that we could just stand still for the rest of eternity, that we could keep what we had, and that it could be perfect.

16

I AWOKE TO screaming. Someone was shaking me.

My eyes snapped open. "Joy?"

"Sarah!" she spluttered, her eyes welling up as she held me by the shoulders. I felt confused and disoriented. How did she get into my dorm room? Why was she so frantic?

"You—I thought you—"

"What's going on, Joy? I—"

"*I thought you'd killed yourself!*" she screamed at me, her hands clenching my shoulders.

The memory of my last text to her rushed back to me. I'd sent it on the chance I never returned from Unreal City, and it certainly had had a feeling of finality to it.

"Your text scared me, and when you didn't reply I came right over. I knocked on the front until someone let me in, and your door was unlocked, and I shook you but you wouldn't wake up and—"

I wrapped my arms around her. "No, no, Joy," I soothed. "That's not what I was doing, at all. Please, don't be upset," I murmured into her ear and to my great surprise, she started crying into my shoulder. I tried to calm her down, my eyes focused on Felix sitting quietly in the corner and watching us with great interest.

"Wh-what happened, then? You were hardly breathing. You wouldn't wake up!" she cried. I pulled away from her, unsure of how to proceed.

"It's—I'm just a heavy sleeper," I tried. Felix laughed from the corner, but Joy looked furious.

"Sarah, I slapped you across the face. I was this close to calling an ambulance. What was going on? Were you on some—some kind of drug?"

No, just poison, I thought as I tried to come up with a satisfactory explanation.

"Tell her, Sarah. Tell her everything," Felix piped up.

Joy tracked my gaze to what she saw as the empty corner, and her concern clearly heightened.

"Sarah, she could be the one. She likes to help people; she'd be grateful for the chance," my familiar prodded.

I shook my head, trying to make it imperceptible to Joy, but she was on to me.

"What are you looking at? Sarah, did you take something weird? Did you have too many pills?"

"Sarah, do it. She'll take the deal. She'll give her blood to the familiar, just like Poe said. If she gives it, we'll all be safe," Felix urged, losing his tone of amusement and looking quite serious.

"No," I said a little too forcefully, and Joy pulled back, thinking I had answered her question in this way.

"I'll reveal myself to her. *I'll* tell her if you don't," Felix threatened, bristling all over. "One of my friends is warped by madness and malice; I can't let him go on in that way."

"*No, Felix! Don't you dare!*" I shouted, getting up from the bed and balling up my fists. Joy's hand covered her mouth as she looked from the corner of the room to where I stood. She shrunk back from me, her eyes huge.

"Sarah, who are you talking to?" she whispered. She must've believed I was completely insane in that moment, but everything changed within seconds.

Felix turned his lamp-like eyes to face Joy, and for one second everything was quiet. Then Joy's scream split the room, and she fell back onto the bed, scrambling backward until she hit the wall.

"*Damn it, Felix!*" I raged. "I thought you weren't allowed to disobey me!?"

"I'm not your familiar, yet. I still possess my own will until then," he snapped back, keeping his eyes fixed on Joy. "I am the reason Sarah would not wake."

"*Wh-what is that thing?!* Sarah! Is it dangerous?!" I could hear Joy's teeth chattering from across the room. I rushed to her side, determined to guard her from anything Felix might be planning.

"I'm not going to hurt you," Felix told Joy. "I just need to tell you what is going on. I need your help."

"Stop right there. Don't you say a word more," I demanded.

Felix's eyes never strayed from his prize. "No, Sarah. If you want to spare her from the truth so badly, then give me your blood and I'll be yours to command for the rest of your life." He had me. I gritted my teeth, trying to order my thoughts, but I couldn't concentrate. Joy's ragged breathing, Felix's agitated purring, the mad pumping of my own heart— my thoughts were scrambled.

"You bastard," was all I could growl out, and Felix proceeded.

"Your friend Sarah was on another plane of reality just now. Her body remained, but her consciousness was in a place she calls Unreal City. It is a world where anything you desire will come to be. I can take her there in return for food," Felix explained to Joy.

Joy didn't seem to know what to think, her expression both terrified and curious. "Is this — is he telling the truth? How can this be real?" She turned to me.

I hesitated to answer, not wanting to lie but refusing to lead her further into his trap. "Yes. As hard as it is to believe, it's all real. But it's not how he makes it sound. It messes you up, it makes you see and feel terrible things, even if it is wonderful, and there's this — "

"There is a great danger that has arisen from that world. Another familiar spirit like me has been...compromised. It has been warped by the malicious emotions of its previous master, and it is the one that is killing. It killed that boy from this school, it killed the other from Sarah's town, and it killed her sister. And it will kill again and again. It needs to be stopped, but in order to do that, it needs blood. It needs a new master," Felix told Joy, his excitement and passion rising until he seemed almost rabid. Joy was shivering, but her eyes remained glued to the spirit.

"That world of wonder, that world where all your dreams can come true. It's waiting for you. You can help all those people. You can stop it. You can put Sarah's poor mind to rest. Just feed it. Feed it blood. Just help it," Felix coaxed her, and I stood up and placed myself between them.

"Don't listen to him, Joy. You don't need to do anything. Please, don't do this. It'll ruin your life. Nothing will ever be the same. You're going to lose part of yourself forever," I pleaded.

"I...I don't understand." Joy was stunned, watching Felix and I shout back and forth at her.

"Joy, you don't understand, he's *evil* — "

"If you don't help it, you could be targeted as the next victim — "

"Everyone stay quiet!" she shouted over us, visibly shaken. She took a shuddering breath as she studied both our faces. The gears in her mind were obviously turning. She took a deep breath and looked at Felix again. "Tell me everything."

My familiar did tell her, but not everything. He stuck to the facts of everything that had happened since I met him down in the caves. I knew that if she heard *everything*, there was no way she would agree to the pact. She wouldn't make the same mistakes I did.

"Just give me a second. Let me think about this." Joy put her face into her hands for what seemed like eons, occasionally lifting her head to check if Felix was still there.

I couldn't take it anymore. "Joy, just let it go. Think of yourself for once. You're not responsible for the lives of strangers —" I started, but she turned irate eyes on me.

"Sarah, how can you say that? You would let all those people get hurt? You would let Lea's death go? What kind of person would I be if I let that happen?"

I continued to shake my head vehemently. "Felix, please stop her."

"No, I — I have to help. I can't let this happen," Joy said, sounding numb as she rose from the bed and approached Felix on wobbly legs.

"You don't have to be a martyr. There's got to be another way!" I screamed, but the more I protested, the more Joy became resolved.

"I'll do it," she proclaimed, looking toward Felix with narrowed eyes.

"I will call him, then," Felix agreed. He flattened back his ears, lifted his head, and opened his mouth. An eerie howl escaped between his jagged teeth like a siren. The noise rattled both of us and we shuddered. The sound stopped, and fear hit me. I cowered, clutching myself.

It's coming, oh God, it's coming…no.

"Felix, what have you done?" I whispered.

His shoulders sank and he looked at me, obviously remorseful yet affirmed in his decision. Joy stood by the window, looking to me with apprehension. I wondered in that moment if she was frightened or regretting what she'd agreed to.

"He's coming. Now, Joy, blood," Felix told her, and hopped onto my desk, taking up the scissors I'd used to cut my hair in his teeth.

"No!" I cried, reaching out to rip the scissors from his mouth.

Felix flashed me a dangerous look that said if I tried to interfere, he wouldn't hesitate to hurt me. He was going to get his way, and I could do nothing to impede him. He leapt off the desk and padded over to Joy, laying the scissors at her feet. She took them up, a soft cry catching in her throat.

I caught her eye and pleaded one last time, "Don't do this." It was my last shot, and I felt a hot tear roll down my cheek.

Our eyes remained connected for a moment longer, and then Joy looked away, pushing her long, dark hair out of her face. She extended her hand and with quivering fingers opened the scissors. She placed either edge of the blades over the plump part of skin on the tip of her pointer finger and took a deep breath. I closed my eyes, unable to watch. I heard the snip, heard her gasp in pain.

When I opened my eyes again, I saw his silhouette at the window. The Antler-Man had come. He waited patiently, waiting for me to invite him in. Felix and Joy's eyes were on me now—expectant, wide, requiring me to make the first move. On the tip of Joy's quivering finger a little droplet of liquid had sprouted, red and bright even in the dimness of the room. With their eyes willing me to move, I knew I'd let him in now or Joy would go out alone to meet him. I couldn't stop her. Even if I prevented her now, she'd do it later. I decided I preferred to be there when it happened, rather than leave her to become lost on her own.

I crossed the room and pulled back the curtain with a violent yank. That face still startled me. He'd been waiting, letting that repulsive drip of water ooze out of his mouth in a steady stream while he drew rattling breaths and scraped his tree-branch hands against the window. Those hollow sunken eyes with their beady pinholes of light beamed at me. The creature's very being exuded an unsoundness of mind that ran even deeper than Poe's had, and it hurt my head to look at him. I looked back to Joy, who'd turned white at the sight of the familiar she was to make a pact with.

"Are you sure about this, Joy? It can never be undone. You've still got time to think it over, we can still—"

"Yes," she said, pushing me aside and wrenching open the window with her uncut hand.

A rush of cold air blustered in, and I hugged myself, trying to restrain my body from rushing forward to tackle Joy out of the way and save her from this fate. I will admit, however, that among my lurches of sickness, a quieter, darker part of myself wanted it. I hated the presence of this feeling in myself, and being aware of it only made the possibility of me becoming ill a more real possibility, but I felt it all the same. I wouldn't be alone anymore. No matter what, Joy would be there. We'd share our sections of the City for the remainder of our days.

Joy extended her quivering hand to the monstrous creature, holding it just beneath its jawless mouth and waited. We watched in suspended terror as the Antler-Man leaned forward and from out of his drain-like mouth slithered a long tongue. I saw Joy's body suffer a tremor, as if she'd almost bolted, but she held firm. That long, fetid, gray thing oozed downward as it bowed its head to drink of Joy's blood. It licked it right off her finger, then drew its tongue back.

Everything seemed to stop in those moments while we all waited for something—anything—to happen. The familiar stared back at us, and at last in a motion that made all three of us jump, he turned and retreated into the woods. We watched him go away from the window, each too stunned to speak until he was long gone and all had become quiet, save the whispering of the wind in the pines.

Joy was the first to move. She fell to her knees, staring at her finger in devastation. I crouched near her, putting a hand cautiously on her back. She looked up at me with those eyes like bright ink and I recognized fear in them. For the second time that night, I cradled her as she cried.

As she clung to me, my eyes went to Felix. He hadn't budged an inch since the spirit had left us. He just kept staring at the open window.

17

JOY AND I didn't sleep that night. After her tears dried, she fell into a state of brief but inconsolable anxiety. I wrapped her up in a blanket from Lea's bed and sat nearby, waiting for her to calm down. The same shock that had ravaged my previous perception of this world was now rattling through her.

Late into the night we talked, and I told her all about my side of the experience since I'd found Felix. The more information about the world I provided for her, the calmer she became. Things are never as scary once they have a name and a set of rules you can play by. I purposefully left out some of the darker details, like when I'd gotten swallowed by the earth and my dismemberment by Poe, in order to keep her grounded. There was no point overwhelming her now when there was still so much to process. And I would protect her from those parts of the City. I had to.

Around dawn, when her questions about my visits to the other world ended, her thoughts turned to her own future.

"So what will happen to me now? Will he come back for me? Will he bring me something that will…take me to that place?" she wondered aloud, staring at the bed sheets. I didn't know what to tell her. I didn't know the answer. I looked to Felix.

"Why did he leave, Felix?" I asked him, and he stayed quiet for a long while.

"I'm not sure. Something was still strange with him. I've never been around another spirit while they recovered from a madness that ran so deeply. I'm not sure how long it will take for her blood to fix him, but if he returns and it worked, he won't look the same. He'll reflect Joy's soul, now. We've got to keep an eye out," he responded.

"Can't you just call him back? Wouldn't that confirm it?"

"I would if I could feel where he is, but he's disappeared. He's gone to Unreal City, I think. He won't be able to hear me from there. I'll let you know when he's returned."

When Joy left the next morning, I felt as if a weight had been shifted inside me, as though the pressure of my enormous secret had been validated as something more than a series of vivid bouts of madness. But it also brought a sense of over-bearing guilt. Though I was grateful that I could share Unreal City with someone whom I had come to care for, I couldn't help but feel that I'd stood by and allowed Joy's life to be stolen from her. She, too, would become addicted to the poison of Unreal City, that intoxicating, infinite power that would efface what we had been told life was all about.

Everything was quiet at last, and I soon fell asleep. Things were safe now. The demon was gone. The sun had risen.

I don't know how long I fell in and out of sleep. I woke to make myself some meager food—often instant noodles. Time lost some of its importance to me. The moon and sun flitted by, and I stayed holed up in my room with Felix. I was too anxious to leave. Midterms came and went. I couldn't bear to face them.

I fed my familiar every time I ate, yet I found it hard to speak to him. I wanted to be furious for what he'd done to Joy, but somehow the furnace inside me that often exploded with an overabundance of anger had gone cold.

The day before Halloween came at last. Joy had to remind me through a series of text messages that we were going on our little adventure southward to Santa Barbara, where the great, salacious festival of drinking and debauchery awaited us. The very idea sickened me. I had no desire to be among that crowd this year, but Joy's boyfriend Kyle was set on going, and she would be accompanying him. I could tell she was still feeling fragile, and because of the mysterious stretch of silence that had followed her pact, I couldn't find it in myself to let her go alone. So I packed my witch's getup and met them at Porter, where we left the mists and redwoods for the central shores.

Joy and I sat in the back during the five-hour drive, and Kyle and his friend David occupied the front of the vehicle. We were going to get into Isla Vista late that night and crash on the floor of his friend's apartment. I didn't mind David so much. He was quiet and absorbed most of Kyle's pedantic rambling so that I was left comfortably to my thoughts. Only a few mild bleed-throughs bothered me on the drive—a feeling of swirling in my chest and a sensation that the walls were closing in on me at one of the rest places we stopped at—but nothing I couldn't handle.

Joy, too, had lost much of her usual talkative nature, and stared out the window for the greater portion of the drive. I remember watching the smooth side of her face and her thick black hair reflecting the pale, reddish light of the sunset while we were driving down the windy highway along the coast. As I watched her, I got the strong urge to start crying again. There was so much I wanted to say to her, but I couldn't—not in the present company. Instead I took hold of her hand for a brief moment. She kept staring out the window, but smiled and squeezed back.

IT WAS WELL after midnight when we arrived in Isla Vista. All I wanted to do was sleep when we pulled up to the apartment, but I was surprised to find Felix waiting at the top of the stairs. I stopped short, looking back at Joy to see if she could see him too. If she could, she gave no sign of it, so I sent him a cross look.

"I thought you might miss me, so I came along," Felix sang as he trotted carefully along the railing. Ignoring him, I followed the rest of our troupe into the apartment.

Inside there were already four or five people gathered around a hookah. The air was thick with incense that seemed to have been burned in an attempt to cover up the odor of garbage that wanted to be taken out. We smoked and drank and talked and stayed up much too late for our own good. Somewhere near dawn, everyone crawled off to their respective corners to try and get some sleep and I wrapped my sleeping bag around me like a protective cocoon and faced the wall. I knew Felix couldn't enter the building until I'd invited him, but I preferred that he keep his distance this night.

We all rose after midday, and went down for a breakfast of the quesadillas the town was famous for. The boys seemed to want to get up to more drinking, but Joy and I decided that we'd rather take a walk than, as one of their friends put it, "pre-game for our pre-gaming". Booming beats were already shaking the ocean village, and Joy complained of a headache, so I suggested we walk down to the beach to clear our heads.

College kids everywhere were already in costume, drinking brazenly in broad daylight. We passed a house where a group of boys had somehow moved a grill and speakers onto the roof and were dancing and cheering at any girls that passed by while they barbequed hot dogs. In the street nearest the beach, a group of young men wearing creepy masks were spiritedly pushing a dumpster they must have commandeered from some alley. Joy and I smirked, but were relieved to reach the sand. It was quieter down there and we at last had a chance to speak candidly.

"Shouldn't something have happened by now, Sarah? Shouldn't it have come back?" she asked me without needing to specify what she meant.

I scratched at the back of my ever-messy hair and sighed. "I don't know. I thought so, too, but I suppose anything could be happening. I guess that's why Felix followed us here, to make sure that—"

"Felix came with us?" she asked, looking at me as worry creased her brows. I matched her frown.

"Yeah, I left him at the apartment. You didn't see him last night?" I asked, dread creeping up on me. She shook her head, and we stared at one another in silence, lost.

"Look, maybe we're just worrying over nothing. We're probably just being paranoid," Joy said in a pinched voice, a ghost of her old smile trying to shine through her worry. "We should just try to have a good time tonight. It'll do us some good."

I gave her an uncertain nod and we sat down together on a large, fallen log between the campus's lagoon and the beach, watching the filthy water flow into the sea through a graffiti-spotted drain. I couldn't help but think of the writing on the wall that led into Poe's garden. My eyes flitted down to the log and I saw a question carved into its worn surface that stirred a feeling of melancholy in my chest.

Will I ever see you again?

Night fell and we returned to the apartment to suit up for our wild night. I shed everything of my usual attire for my witch's robes, but kept my necklace on. Though I'd tried not to dwell on her since my last visit to Unreal City, I still thought of Lea. I wondered if she would've been here with me right now, perhaps wearing a matching costume, perhaps supporting both Joy and I through this. As I put the silly hat onto my head, I wondered if she'd known what was killing her at the moment of her death. Had she been able to see the familiar, or was it invisible to her as Felix had been to Joy last night? Or had she looked into its jar and felt her throat fill with water, choking her last breath as she was terrorized by its twisted appearance? The old furnace inside me lit up as I did my makeup. Who had done it? Whose familiar had it been? Who had wanted to kill Lea, or Poe, or me for that matter? I would never get to know now that Joy had claimed the familiar as her own. This tore at my mind until a thought occurred to me.

Do they keep their memories from when they were with their previous masters?

With this question nagging at me, I excused myself and went out onto the balcony where Felix waited. Now that night had fallen, the town was rumbling with the sounds of raucous partying and hooting cries of merrymaking in the streets. Felix blinked at me as I walked up to him.

"Can familiars remember the times from when they belonged to another master?" I asked bluntly.

"Yes."

"So when Joy's familiar finally appears to her she would be able to ask it why it killed Lea. Right? It would know everything, right?" I chewed my lip, and he paused for a long while before nodding. I exhaled and looked out at the horizon to where the ocean was. I was so close to knowing.

And what would it be like when I did? Would I be able to let her go, as I had been instructed to do? Would I be freed or would I be crushed? Would I have the courage to tell my mother and father why they would never see their daughter again? Would they *want* to know? Of course Mom would want to know; she was the one who still waited every day to see if Lea's boyfriend would wake from his coma and explain the details about the night she was murdered—and what he would tell them would sound like the ravings of a lunatic. Of course, I too would appear unsound of mind if I ever tried to explain the truth.

These manic musings were interrupted as Joy came out in her nurse costume and motioned me back inside. We were all going to take our first shots of the night, then try to lose ourselves in the frenzy of the wicked holiday. Whiskey passed my lips; I felt it burn in my stomach. The mood didn't lighten, but intensified. My laugh sounded like the bark of an agitated dog in my ears, but I laughed nonetheless. We took to the streets, determined to fight our way through the teeming crowd in order to find our way to the street nearest the beach, where many of the parties we'd promised to visit were being held.

My head was spinning in a world of brilliant color and grotesque faces. Masks grinned, bloodied faces loomed, eyes crinkled and mouths widened, warped in the middle of screeching laughter. The howls of drunken ghouls echoed through the streets and chilled me more than any of the displays of gore adorning people's bodies. Green lights, orange lights, purple lights. Naked torsos and bare thighs caught my eyes. Smooth, plump thighs. Sex and violence filled every corner of this town. We fought our way through the dancing, pushing bodies that packed the streets. Every so often I glanced down to see that Felix still followed me and felt comforted by his eyes. They seemed to anchor me to everything. I could hear roaring now, and I wasn't sure if it was a bleedthrough or some effect of the night.

We arrived at our first house and a French maid greeted us. More alcohol flowed into me—tequila, vodka and orange juice, beer…I stopped keeping track. The room was spinning now, but I didn't feel sick. I just kept laughing my barking laugh, my gaze fixed on Felix, with occasional glances to see if Joy was having fun. Even while everything else was spinning, he seemed to always be standing still while he watched me— half-protective, half-hungry.

We went on to the next party, and the next, making our way down the road and getting drunker and drunker. Everyone was laughing now. We'd gotten caught up in the wonderful, terrible hive-mind of the town. This was fun. This was what youth was all about. Another hostess greeted us, another pair of half-exposed breasts stole everyone's eyes. Another drink? *Sure.* If it's there, why not? This is what living was all about. We started playing a game, but I couldn't figure out the rules. Joy looked like she was really enjoying herself though, and that made me glad. My stomach burned with anger, however, when Kyle started kissing her on the neck. I stared at them for a minute, then forced myself to look away. It disgusted me. A girl to my left was offering me a pill, and I shook my head as the feeling of nausea became overpowering.

No pills, thanks, only poison for me.

I was going to be sick. I got up without saying anything and made my way outside with Felix at my heels. Now that I was away from the music, my ears hummed. I wondered if they turned it up that loud to eliminate the need for conversation. Did we all have that little to say? We were close to the end of the street now, and I could see the ocean in the distance. Beyond the edge of the asphalt was an expanse where tall grasses grew and a dirt trail led off into the darkness. Out there I could see monstrously large dandelions waving in the breeze, and for a moment I was hypnotized by them. I knew they were just another bleed-through, but I found them beautiful all the same.

Joy and Kyle came out to check on me after a few minutes. I assured them that I was fine, just in need of fresh air. As I went through the motions of getting them to leave me alone so I could be sick in peace, something standing among the dandelions caught my eye. At first I thought it was a trick of the light, but I turned my head in horror when it didn't fade.

He was there, watching us—the Antler-Man. At once I couldn't breathe, and I stood staring at it, feeling the blood drain from my face. He was the same. He was still that hideous, malformed, spindly thing with his dripping jawless mouth and beady eyes. Joy followed my gaze, then turned back to me in confusion.

"Sarah, is everything all right?" she asked, and I knew that she could not see him. Something had gone very wrong.

*Come to Unreal City…*his voice growled in my head, resonating inside of me. *I miss you. I need you. Come back to me.*

"Ev—" I took a moment to catch my breath and kept my face straight. "Everything is fine. I just don't feel well. I'll be back in a minute, I promise," I breathed, not daring to take my eyes off the Antler-Man even for a second. Joy looked there again, and I was sure now. The pact had never been made between them. It hadn't worked. Something had misfired.

"Okay, if you say so. Hurry back." Joy wobbled back into the house, but Kyle remained.

"What's so interesting over there, huh?"

"Nothing, leave me alone."

"You're psychotic, you know that? Joy feels sorry for you; that's why she invited you to this. You need medication," Kyle said decisively, and I think he actually meant to be helpful with this little nugget. I turned to him, hoping my dislike of him shone as clearly in my eyes as I felt it in my heart.

"One day, a long time from now, you're going to be deeply ashamed of who you are right now. In the meantime, however, you can go fuck yourself," I snarled and he drew back, his lip curling.

"You—"

"Get outta my face." I stomped away from him and toward the familiar, the fear in the back of my chest nullified by the anger I felt for everything. It wasn't just Kyle. It was my entire circumstance. It was losing Lea. It was the disillusionment of the brief moment of security I'd felt knowing that Joy would be with me forever in Unreal City being undone by this familiar's presence. Felix bristled as I made my way toward the Antler-Man.

"What are you doing?" he called after me.

"I'm gonna go talk to him. I'm gonna find out everything I want to know." My voice trembled, but I kept on walking, the wind ripping at the loose gown fluttering around my knees.

"He'll kill you!" Felix hissed, but I wouldn't be swayed.

"I don't care." The alcohol made me believe I was invincible, constricting the fear that often crushed me when this abomination was near. I crossed from the asphalt onto the grasslands, getting closer by the second.

"*Lea, please stop!*"

This time I did stop. I turned my back on the familiar to stare at Felix, incredulous. An epiphany struck like a bolt of lightning. All at once, everything made sense.

18

"YOU WERE HER familiar, weren't you?" I stammered, staring at Felix as my heart smashed against my ribs. "You made a pact with Lea, didn't you?"

"I—" Felix's pupils had become slits and his toothy jaw hung open. He hung his head and murmured out a pathetic little, "Yes."

"God damn it, Felix—" I crumpled, losing my will to keep going toward the Antler-Man. I knew he was still behind me, I knew he was waiting and watching, but I couldn't get up the energy to care anymore. My brain tried to think, tried to make the connections, but was impaired by the staggering amount of alcohol I'd consumed.

"Then you know everything. You were there. You know why—why was she killed?" I demanded. Felix's eyes flitted to the area behind me where the lunatic familiar waited, but he made his way through the tall grass toward me.

"That night, my friend's master was upset, and he ordered his spirit to hurt all those who'd wronged him."

"Lea never hurt *anyone*! How dare you!" I screamed, suddenly not wanting to know what he had to say. From behind me, I heard the Antler-Man give a roar that made the whole sea-cliff tremble. I whimpered and covered my head while I waited out the tremor.

Come back to Unreal City. Come find me. Come back to me!

"Let me finish, Sarah!" Felix sounded urgent. I could tell from his fixed stare over my shoulder and the way his fur bristled that the Antler-Man was coming. "His master's command was so full of malice, so corrupted by his hatred that his state of mind was altered. While he moved to destroy the boy who had tormented him, Lea tried to stop him. She got in his way, absorbed the blow and perished in her attempt to stop him."

"Who would ever — who would do such a — " And again, for the second time that night, my subconscious fit everything together in a moment of blinding clarity. "Stephen. It was Stephen."

"Yes, Sarah, now please, we've got to get out of here. He's coming for you, he — "

"Of course it was him. And that's why Joy's blood didn't work. It's because he's still *alive*. He's in a coma, he's — " I sputtered, putting my hands to my forehead. "He's in Unreal City. He's been dreaming there this whole time."

"Yes, Sarah. Stephen lost his mind when he saw he'd killed Lea, and warped my friend's mind in doing so. The master and servant are connected; you saw Poe's familiar. But what you must understand is that Stephen's not just in his garden dreaming. He's trapped in the deep place under the City. He can't get out. His familiar wanders the places between this world and the other, searching for him — tortured by his hunger, trying desperately to carry out his master's wishes in hopes that he'll come back. He kills indiscriminately, acting upon his master's malice, which arose from those who berated him, and he searches endlessly for your sister. Neither will accept that she's gone, and that's why they're drawn to you—it's why *I* was drawn to you. You're carrying her around your neck, Sarah," Felix sputtered.

"You never told me *any of this!? WHY?*" I yelled, clutching the pendant around my neck.

"You never *ask—*"

"Bullshit, you've broken enough rules to—"

"Sarah, this is hardly the time or place. We need to get inside, we need to—"

The howl of the Antler-Man split the night again, growing so loud I thought my eardrums would burst. Tears sprang to my eyes as the sound shook my body and I cowered, but then it all faded. I looked behind me to find the Antler-Man had gone.

"Where is he?" I whispered to Felix, looking around the cliff.

"I—I don't know. He's still on this side of reality, but—" he paused and looked up at me with remorse. I stood up, my legs feeling weak and my head still spinning from intoxication. I could feel him too; he'd gone closer to the sea. He was waiting for me, waiting to bring me to his master. I took a step in his direction and Felix gave a pathetic little meow. I turned back to him.

"How could you keep all this from me?" I demanded, my voice cracking.

"My mistake was believing that my friend had detached himself from Stephen's spirit. I honestly thought it would reassign itself to Joy when it tasted her blood and—"

"No, that has nothing to do with this. Why did you keep *everything* from me?" I protested, and he hung his head.

"For the same reason Stella and Angus and all the others kept it from you. We all loved Lea. She was kind. Her dreams were beautiful, and her soul was pure. She was so unlike many of the masters I've had, and we all hoped that she would stay forever. We didn't want you to fall to the same fate. We wanted to keep you from dying the way she did. I thought if you never knew, you'd never go looking for him. But it seems he found you, instead."

"You wanted to keep me alive cause I *look* like her, or – or sound like her? Like, what, am I Lea's substitute? Is that it?"

"No, Sarah, because your heart is just as pure, and you're just as kind. You try and cover it up with your rage and misery to keep yourself from caring about people, and to keep people from caring about you. You're scared to death of losing anyone else, so you just try to stop caring, but that's not *you*. That's not your soul. I know because I've seen it, and it's just as beautiful as Lea's was," Felix purred. "When my master is cruel, my world is cruel, and the number of good people is in short supply. I wanted to keep you as my master for as long as I could. It was selfish, but then I don't love anything as much as I love myself. I apologize for misleading you." Felix bowed his head and crept closer.

I had the sudden urge to hurt him, to kick him away as hard as I could – maybe because he was so vulnerable or I was so angry – but it passed quickly. I felt the truth ringing for the second time in my life, like Mom had promised me I would feel, and dropped down to my knees. I opened my arms to him.

He crawled onto my knees and I curled my arms around him. I held him like someone might hold to the side of a tree as a great wind blew by. With shivering fingers, I stroked his fur and felt his throat quivering as he purred against my arm.

"I understand. I understand why you did it, but you know I can't just let this go on. I've got to set things right. Stephen was my friend, too. Lea loved him, and to leave him the way he is – trapped down there – I won't allow it. How do I get to him?" I asked, and his purring stopped abruptly.

"You've got to get at him to help him, and that's almost impossible. He's buried beneath his garden, just like you almost were," Felix said, sounding quite put-out. I contemplated this and something occurred to me. The diamond knife that I'd cried out, tear by tear, on the cliff. That man had told me it was a tool.

"I think I know how. You've got to send me there. Take me to Unreal City," I begged and he leapt out of my lap, regarding me with his burning eyes.

"You'll lose your mind down there."

I held firm. "I don't care. Send me."

"Feed me then," he relented, though his voice was darker than I expected it to be. He was usually so gleeful at the mention of food. I reached to yank out some hair, but he shook his head. "No more fooling around, Sarah. You want me to let you risk your life. You've got to pay up. I've given you more than enough time to decide. If you're serious about this, then show me," he demanded.

I hesitated. If I lived through this, would this be the life that I'd want to come back to? Would I want to be bound to this creature for as long as I lived—a bond deeper than anything the human mind could dream up? Trapped in each other's care and company, with insanity and delusion as my regular bedfellows? But I could also have the world, and more. I could be the master of my own infinity, the despot of my own solipsistic universe. Unlimited, even by the edges of my own imagination. Bound forever to the elite few who dared to dream further than the common man could ever conceive. Yes, it appealed to me; it appealed to the best and worst parts of me. And I decided in that instant that I could live with that sort of violent ecstasy. I was only ever guaranteed this one life, no matter what the faithful promised. I might as well make it spectacular.

"All right," I surrendered. "I'm yours."

19

THE BITE HURT more than I expected it would. Felix crawled his way up my body and sank his sharp, digging teeth into the side of my neck. I whimpered and sank downward, feeling the pulse of pain resonate through me. My skin grew hot as he retracted his teeth and lapped at the spots of blood oozing out of the puncture wounds. His tongue was rough on the open wounds, and I gave a sob each time he licked. Felix seemed to go into a frenzy once he tasted my blood, but when he'd had his fill after about five minutes he bounced off me and paced around my legs, licking his lips. I waited to feel some profound sense of bonding with him, or any indicator at all really, but nothing happened. The pact had been made quietly, without the slightest ripple of disturbance. How easy it could be to make this mistake if one didn't know what they were getting into.

"It's done. I'll be here for the rest of your life, though if you're determined to go through with what you're planning, I'm not sure how long that will be. The promise we made before still stands, you know. If you lose your mind down there, I'll have to kill you. I'm bound by my word now, unless you order me differently."

"I know," I told him, rubbing at the side of my neck and drawing my hand back to look at the blood spatters on my fingers. "But I'm determined. Let's go. Now, before I lose my nerve." I felt like electric currents were shooting up my spine, alight with the sense of oncoming danger.

Felix spun in place, causing my intoxicated head to whirl even more violently. He stopped and that little box sat under his paws, waiting for me. I pulled it up off the ground and consumed its contents. The enchanting flavor hit me, making me forget everything for the duration of its blissful passing. I sank down into the tall grass and closed my eyes, waiting to lift away from my earthly bonds. Because I was anticipating it with such urgency this time around, it wasn't so much a pleasant drifting sensation as it was a rocket upwards. I felt like I'd boarded a ride at an amusement park—one that shoots up at an incredible speed before dropping, though the drop never came. I just kept hurtling into the sky, past the edges of the world. I tried to see what was going on around me, but there were only jets of very bright light surrounding me. I opened my mouth to call for Felix's help and found I could make no sound.

I kept trying to shout for him until I could hear my own voice again, whistling through the air. As vision returned to me, I found that I wasn't resting peacefully in the beds of clover and moss of my garden, but miles above Unreal City and dropping toward it with increasing velocity. My witch's hat was caught in the wind and flew away. Eyes streaming, I looked around again to see Felix falling beside me.

"*This is why you wait for me to lead you here!*" he howled over the roar of the wind and all I could do was nod in agreement. I could see all twelve gardens arranged on the disc. I guessed I had about four minutes before impact, and tried to ride the currents and aim for my garden where the landing was sure to be safe. I noticed my left hand held the diamond knife that I'd created on my previous visit.

Use it to defend yourself. Use it to get to the deep place. That was what he'd told me to do. I grasped the dagger's hilt with both hands and glanced about.

"Felix, which garden in Stephen's?" I shouted to him. He swam his way over to me, hooking onto the back of my robes.

"The eleventh. That one that looks dead, there."

It was difficult to distinguish which one he was describing. I saw two gardens that appeared to be barren landscapes from this high above the world, but I soon could tell them apart by the spurts of lightning and the warped, craggy hills of Poe's domain. My eyes narrowed and I kept my vision focused on the arid earth of the garden between the tranquil beach of the Japanese fisherwoman and the heather-dotted plains of the man with the Kelpie. With the point of my dagger aiming directly at that hard, baked dirt, I flew toward it with determination and confidence that I would break it apart, and not the other way around.

I expected a violent crash, or a vicious thud at the very least as I neared the ground. In the split second before impact, deep panic and doubt shot through me. Why had I done this? How could I have been sure? But with my arm extended in front of me, the point of the dagger touched the ground before any part of my body, stabbing through with ease, as though it were the surface of a balloon rather than hard-packed dirt.

I gave a victorious shout as the world formed into a concave shape and I was pulled through a chute of darkness. I called out for Felix but could not hear his voice. Down, down I went.

I couldn't see a thing at first. I just kept falling. I couldn't feel the presence of any familiars, other Cunning Folk, the life-hum of the gardens, or anything at all. Just empty space. I fell down the chute, daunted at what I might find at the bottom of it. And then I saw earth, roots, and a meager light coming from the clusters of minerals embedded in them.

Soon I could see things buried in the sides of the tunnel. I saw jars pushed into the earth, like the ones often used to preserve jam. The light in here was coming from inside of them, not the minerals. There were images inside, each with their own feeble luminescence, and I could see the forms of people moving, talking, and just living their everyday lives. Once or twice I thought I saw my own face — or was it Lea's? — inside one of those jars, but I was falling too fast to be sure. I saw other things: brass keys, the bones of a small dog, coils, beads, threads, pages from a book, a burnt polaroid…the more I looked at them, the sadder I became, and eventually I closed my eyes and allowed myself to be consumed by the sensation of the fall.

Then, little by little, that sensation weakened until I realized that I wasn't falling anymore. I opened my eyes again and saw that I lay at the bottom of a cavern in the shadow of a pair of massive statues. They were wreathed in torches; a dramatic, flickering light that made their tortured faces almost come alive. The figures looked like ogres, but human in shape. Each held a spear and assaulted one another with their weapon, stabbing each other's heart. The left one's face looked mad with fright and the right one deeply miserable.

I rose to my feet, fixated on the statues. In between them was a pathway: the cavern went even deeper. I approached the statues, my dread increasing, half expecting them to burst to life and skewer me. With careful steps, I crossed under the portal they created with their curved arms and torsos and once again passed into darkness.

The temperature began to drop. I shivered, holding tightly to myself as the hairs on my arms and neck stood up. The further I went, the more intolerable it got. It seemed as though I was making my way through an arctic tundra. Fingers and toes stung with that painful sort of numbness only severe cold can bring.

Spotting another torch in the distance, I picked up my pace. It hung upon a brick wall and behind it I sensed a pounding disturbance. I screeched to a halt, but a little too late. A long, pale arm with black, decaying fingernails ripped through the solid brick and seized the front of my robe, pulled me against the wall and wrapped around my shoulders. As I tried to pull away, more hands exploded through the wall and grasped me from head to toe, swarming me with dirty, rotting fingernails and white, clammy skin—waterlogged skin. They bashed my cold-numbed limbs, creeping over every inch of my body, pulling me deeper and deeper into the walls until all I could feel was the surging of bones and flesh. I couldn't breathe. Fingers were wiggling in my mouth, scratching at my eyes, digging into my ears, ripping out my hair.

I somehow reached the other side of this, and they thrust me away at once. I staggered forward, a bloody and beaten mess, only to crash into a set of rusty iron bars. Somehow I'd been trapped in a cage through the chaos of those surging hands. I could see beyond the bars that many other cages surrounded me, and inside of them all were people—people with kind eyes, young people, beautiful people, children and gentle old folks. But they all cowered in fear at the things moving between our cages, things that appeared monstrous to me. I, too, cringed and followed the examples of the other captives, moving as far away from the creatures outside of the cages as I could.

Through the lattice of my own fingers I dared to look upon the infernal beasts. They were horrific to behold, not quite animal, not quite human. They had attributes of primal things, of things that existed before names and understanding. I saw parts of insects, of crustaceans, of things from the dark places of the earth. Things that lived in total darkness and fed upon the detritus of life.

Yet they smiled and laughed like an intoxicated mob at a carnival, much like I had just an hour ago at Halloween parties. Some were half-formed, and others were torn apart, but all were reveling in the torment of the innocents behind the bars. I, too, had become one of many trapped victims. I was one more toy for the unlimited, curious cruelty of this world.

Things were burning somewhere close. There was screaming. Something was being roasted on a spit—something that once had eyes.

Will no one help them? Will no one help us?

Below my feet was a heap of bones, and between them through the sockets and ribs crawled dark things. I could see some of my fellow victims being heaved into a pit of white-hot flame. Nothing was spatial, just terrible images, stretching on forever in this disproportionate expanse that wouldn't apply to the rules of scientific structure. And some victims were drowning. The drowning, the drowning was the worst, sinking deeper into black water, coughing sputtering, choking. Some music grew loud now, off-tune and grinding into my ears, and the more I looked around, the more I came to understand that all of this was happening inside of one, huge being: one living entity with parts of his body caved out and turned into structures and—

You're losing it, Sarah, rang a voice from inside of my head. It wasn't my voice, though it sounded so similar. *None of this is real. The longer you look, the deeper it goes, and soon you'll become a part of it for good.* I could feel electricity course within the region of my chest, and it cleared my mind, washing away the ache and horror from witnessing so much suffering. And then they were coming at me again, with their wild eyes and sharp teeth and weapons raised.

"STOP!" I screamed, and drove my dagger into the ground. When the knife's point hit the pile of bones, the dagger broke apart, exploding into a thousand shards of light and tearing apart the hellish vision before me.

It wiped the chaos from existence in one brilliant conflagration of light that burned my eyes. When the luminous flash faded, I could feel I was standing just above the deepest part of the City now. I could feel it working and turning and moving and changing beneath my feet, yet all I could see was that I was inside a little sphere of silvery metal and that *he* was there with me.

He was sleeping, in a bed also made from that shining, bright metal as he lay among sheets of gossamer and silk. He looked peaceful, unaware of where he was or what was happening around him—or because of him. But he also looked sad, as if he was dreaming of a happier time that he knew, in the far reaches of his mind, was his ruined paradise.

"Stephen," I said as I drew near him, his face and features so familiar to me. He looked just as he did when I'd last seen him in the hospital, the same dark, unkempt hair, the same pale skin and sharp features. It was that face that always made Lea light up when she saw him coming up the driveway. He wouldn't wake when I said his name, so I sat beside him on the bed and shook his shoulder. With some effort he began to stir and opened his eyes.

"Lea, Lea," he whispered, rising and clutching my shoulders, eyes alight with rapture. "Oh, God, I had such a terrible dream!"

"Stephen, look closer," I said. "It's me, not Lea."

"What?" He squinted at my face. "No, no it's you. I know it's you. It's got to be."

"No, wake up, look at me," I said, taking his face in my hands and staring into his eyes. "See? Not Lea."

"You...you're right," he breathed, and I sighed as I lowered my hands and gave him a sad smile.

"Sarah. But this is—" He looked around and started to get his bearings, memories clearly coming back to him. "This is Unreal City, isn't it? Only we're—"

"Below it," I finished for him and once again I had his attention. "You've been trapped down here for months, Stephen. You can't wake up. You're in a coma."

He couldn't seem to digest this. "No, no, this can't be right. This can't be Unreal City if you're here, unless Lea told you? She wanted to from the beginning, you know, but I made her promise not to. This place was supposed to be for *us*." He sounded distasteful at the thought, but my chest seized with emotion. My sister had wanted to share this with me....

"No, Stephen," I heard my voice warble and steeled it with all my might. "Can't you remember what happened?"

A wave of darkness passed over his face and he dropped his eyes to the gossamer bedspread. "The last thing I remember is—is we were in town. That asshole from school—Isaac—was following me around, shouting things at me, threatening me, and I was mad. Lea made him go away and we walked all night talking about it. I was still upset and then I saw him again and—"

"That was back in June. It's almost November now," I said quietly, throat catching as I thought of what I had to say next. I knew how it felt to have that kind of weight just thrown onto you. I'd heard it from a stranger, a policeman who came and went as if he were the one that had taken Lea from us. It was unthinkable to have someone you hardly knew deliver the news that the most important part of your life had just been erased... to have that person see you screaming, to have that person witness you fall to pieces bit by bit. "You've been sleeping."

"That long?" He seemed stunned.

It was hard to believe Stephen had done this. I knew he'd had a rough time in school, but he was always so gentle with Lea and my family. Yes, he'd been into weird stuff, things that made my parents' eyebrows raise when Lea told them about him, but I always thought it was just a front. I never thought he'd had it in him to be so malicious.

A shadow crossed his expression as more of his memories returned. "He's dead, isn't he? Isaac? I ordered Elk to kill him, to kill them all, all the ones who were making good people's lives miserable. He really did it, didn't he?"

"Y-yes, Stephen, your familiar has hurt, well, a lot of people now. He's sick, I think, that's why I came here, to try and help him and you. Why did you do it? Why?"

"Because I'd had enough of their bullshit!" he shouted with such fury that I finally glimpsed the part of him that was capable of such an act. Something in his eyes changed in that moment. "They break people down for fun. They ruin people's lives, picking off the weak ones just because they can, just because they're *bored*." Stephen was frantic now, rambling and shivering with fervid rage.

"They made my life unbearable, so full of shame and hate and—it was all I could remember. They started on me when I was a kid, *just a kid*. I was hounded, degraded—cornered and attacked. And trash like Isaac—he didn't deserve to live. Not after what he put me and everyone else he targeted through. Him and that bastard Poe. That sadistic fuck. He tried to hurt me. He came to my garden and threatened us. Called Lea things—*horrible things*. You would've done the same if you'd heard." Stephen's eyes were wild and I shrunk back from him. This wasn't the same boy I'd known, not at all. His ranting grew into a manic, screaming tirade.

"And I *know* it wasn't just them, either, there are thousands of them. They *torture* all the people who they don't see as equal and I thought—I thought who will help them? Of course it had to be me. I could put a stop to them for good. Bring justice, free all the innocent people Isaac tormented. And rid Unreal City of filth like Poe. I had the power to make this world *better*, to get the bad guys. I thought I could be a hero and I'd been thinking about it for a while. After Isaac found us that night and started talking to Lea the way he did I just—"

"But did you have to *kill* them, Stephen?" I couldn't stop myself, and instantly regretted it. Stephen's eyes grew very wide and he stepped closer, an accusatory finger pointed at me.

"See that's the problem with this world, that's just it. You're the problem. No one understands. You don't know what I've been through. My first memory is of getting sand thrown in my face in kindergarten. They just *picked* me. They thought the way I reacted was funny, they thought my anger and pain and terror was *funny*. So they kept it up, and it got worse and worse through the years. I can't tell you how many times I've been beat up for entertainment, degraded—for their *amusement! I couldn't leave my house without feeling scared for my safety and it was a game to them!*" He was shrieking now and poking me hard. I slapped his hand away, but he grabbed me by the front of my shirt.

"And you want to know why *you're* the problem, Sarah? You want to know why?"

"Let me go! Stop it, Stephen!"

"Because every time I went to someone like *you* for help—a teacher, my parents, a counselor, a campus supervisor, *the police*—anyone who had the power to stop them they would do...*nothing*. Sure, they give it a token try because they had to, but they never saved me. They always came back to laugh at me. They kept me in my cage. Those monsters got away with what they did because they were good at keeping their hands clean. No one but Lea would help me! No one. And *they got away with it!*"

As I beheld all the fury and anguish within his desperate eyes, my brain made a connection. That hell-scape I'd seen, the one I'd broken with my knife, wasn't Unreal City itself. It was still Stephen's garden. Those creatures swarming with all those vile displays of cruelty—those were *his* demons. That was how he felt almost every day of his life. His life had gone that far out of his control, and he'd been given unlimited power—the power to finally stop all that pain. I could almost understand him. I knew then what to say, how I could get through to him.

"I'm sorry, Stephen, I'm sorry that happened to you. I can feel why you'd want to see them pay for what they did to you. But you have to know that's not what she would've wanted. That's not what she wanted, was it? She—" I pressed gently, trying to jog his memory. From the look of despair that coursed through his expression I figured the memory of that night was starting to come back. He let me go, his anger deflating.

"No, she tried to stop him, she—she—and Aoife was yowling too and—"

"Who?"

"Lea's familiar, she looks like a white cat with bright blue eyes. You must've seen her now if Lea told you…she must've brought you here, that's why you're here and Lea is—" Stephen was starting to sound frantic and I held up my hand to stop him.

"Lea's dead, Stephen. She died trying to stop you," I whispered, taking his hand as I saw his face go white. "That's why you shut down. You've been down here, unable to accept that."

"*No!*" His scream shook the very walls and it was like a tremor had moved the ground. I almost lost my balance and fell off the bed, but steadied myself, keeping my eyes fixed on him. I could tell by the tears sliding down his cheeks that he knew it was true; he just didn't know what to say. "No, this… this can't be…this wasn't the way it was supposed to happen.

I—" He stopped, his eyes turning cold and severe. "I don't believe you."

"Stephen, please—"

"*ELK!*" he cried to the ceiling. He called the name of his familiar again and again, and for a moment I thought it was all in vain until I spotted a drip of viscous water coming from the top of the sphere we were trapped inside. I shrunk back from the pool the drips were forming on the floor, terrified to be trapped in this small space with the Antler-Man.

Stephen watched my aversion with intense, searching eyes. Bit by bit, drop by drop, Elk formed until he stood above us, tall and crooked with the tips of his antlers pushing up against the inner curves of the sphere. For the longest, tensest of moments, Stephen was at a loss for words.

"Elk. Elk what happened to you? You changed. You... you're different. You look like you're rotting. What've you done, Elk?" Stephen murmured.

"Your bidding. I've done your bidding. Purge the world of the undeserving. Find her. I've brought her to you. See? See? Won't you feed me now? I'm dying master, I'm dying!"

"No, no!" Stephen cried, throwing the bed sheets off and standing. He was hardly half his familiar's height. "You've ruined *everything*. You murdered her!"

"She decided her own fate. She stepped in the way. Suicide. There was nothing I could do to prevent it," he breathed through his fetid hole of a throat. "It was you that brought about this undoing of lives. I was merely the tool in your hand."

"You'll pay for what you did! You'll pay, you'll pay!" he raged at the familiar and went to throw a punch. I cried out and tried to catch his arm, but was too late to stop him.

The familiar put up its tree branch hands and caught his fist before it could connect. Stephen yelped as his familiar's hands curled around him, his finger-like appendages snaking around Stephen's arms like roots, spreading over his entire body. He was screaming as the familiar leaned forward and lifted the boy into the air. The creature's mouth opened wide and he tilted his head back as it stretched wider.

He swallowed his master. Elk's skin bulged outward to fit Stephen's body inside his emaciated form. I stumbled backward, stunned. Stephen's wriggling form was melting bit by bit inside the familiar's engorged belly as pools of water dripped from its mouth and out the hole of the vat.

As the creature digested Stephen and the thrashing within his belly stopped, Elk's body began to transform. He sprouted several leg-like limbs from the top of his back and his hair grew like weeds. A snout formed, lined with fangs, and those little pinhole eyes became great, bulging spheres of dark yellow, red, and green. This was no longer Elk. The being roared at me and I shrunk back as its many legs curled around the sides of the room.

I was awed by the sight of it—so terrible and full of hatred and anger. There was nothing I could do, nowhere I could run. My diamond knife had broken and disappeared. I was weak here, crushed by the pressure of being so deep under the ground. There was no exit this deep under the City. I couldn't get out.

I can't fight this. I can't even fend it off. There's no way around it. Bolts of understanding shot through me and I stared at the revolting sight, but I already understood what I needed to do to get out of this. *There's no way around it, and if I can't run from it, and I can't kill it, then I just have to go through it.*

I knew analyzing it would stop me in my tracks, and without hesitation I leapt up, reaching for its jaws. It snarled at me, hooked its teeth into my arms, and—just as I suspected—began to suck me down its throat. I squeezed my eyes shut and felt myself slide down the stinking, slimy chute into its stomach. I became completely submerged in the fluid—I was drowning, disappearing, being assimilated.

I opened my eyes as I was tossed about inside the creature's body, and was surprised to see a light floating in front of me. It was weak, bluish-purple in color, the color of lightning, coming from my necklace. From the light of this glow, I could see that Stephen was still there, floating beside me.

"I never meant for this to happen, Sarah. I'm sorry. I'm sorry for everything," he said, though his mouth never moved.

"I know," I spoke back in the same way. "None of this was supposed to happen the way it did. It wasn't the life we were promised, the one we hoped would come true. But it's the way things turned out. It happened."

"Lea was everything to me. She was my light – she protected me from the ones who were against me – and from myself. She showed me how good the world could be. She gave me hope. I can't – I can't accept that I was the one that –"

"I know," I repeated, feeling my heart ache because of him, and for him. "She was the same thing to me. She was to so many."

"You must think I'm a monster. I took her from you. You must hate me."

"I feel for you. Anyone who lives through the same pain that I do – I couldn't possibly hate. There's already enough pain, as it is," I told him tenderly. "I forgive you."

He groaned, his grief causing him to shrivel up. I reached through the darkness and murky water until I caught hold of his hand. Instantly the little light from my necklace faded and we were left there, drowning but undying in the dark. It seemed to last forever, but then I felt his hand squeeze mine.

"I think…I think I can still set this right. Or at least try to undo some of the damage," he murmured. He was quiet for a moment, and I waited to see what he would do. "Elk, if you're still there, if some part of you can still hear me, I need you to do something for me. Set me free. Let this all end. If I'm gone, the part that's making you want to hurt others might be gone, too. Go on and set me free."

"Stephen, no, there's got to be another way."

Just then the body that entrapped us both shuddered a great sigh. We were shaken about as the shiver grew more violent, and then everything was heating up around us, boiling us. The heat seemed to be erasing everything from below us, and it was rising, reverting everything back to the way it had once been. I called over and over for Stephen and clawed around in the pitch black water all around me, but he was gone. As the temperature reached an intensity that was sure to melt away my body, things again became still, and the heat dissipated. My sense of the spirit enclosing me vanished, as did any notion that Stephen was near me. This garden was empty.

I TRIED TO howl out my frustration and terror, but only a jet of water issued from my mouth. I was trapped here now. Stephen's wish had been granted. The familiar had probably gone back to the other side of reality and taken the life of his master. The poison had been drawn from the wound — the toxic earth had been made clean again. The familiar was probably free too, roaming the Earth again in the shadowy places and looking for a new master. I could feel it because the substance I was floating in now wasn't the filthy, acidic mixture of its stomach, but clear and clean water. But if this garden belonged to no one, now, what was to become of me?

Keeping my panic at bay, I waited. I waited for hours in silence, hoping against all hope that I would wake from this dream as I always did and drift back to my body. But I did not. I stayed suspended in my watery prison. I tried to find the perimeter, and could find neither top nor bottom nor sides. It went on forever. Gripped by despair, I pulled my knees to my chest and began to sob. This was it. I was in too deep to escape. There wasn't any way out. Even if another master came to this garden and brought it back into life, how could they know where I was? How could they dig me out of here, even if they did? I thought of Felix, starving as my body would sleep endlessly. I wondered if he could even feel me down here.

Desperation spiked in my heart, and I tried calling to him. I screamed with whatever voice I could muster, but the longer I called, the deeper my despair grew. With a darkening heart, I realized that I couldn't even take the easy way out as Stephen had. I would have to wait until some natural death came to my body on Earth before I was able to escape. I hugged my knees tighter to my chest, wracked with anguish. They would probably think I collapsed from alcohol poisoning when they found me. I would be put into the hospital just as Stephen had, kept alive by machines and intravenous fluid. Would Felix stay by my side, poised in wait to see if I ever awoke, or perhaps creep between the gardens of the Unreal City in search of my lost spirit? Would Joy weep for me? Would my parents have any strength left to go on after losing another daughter?

I don't know how long I stayed down there; time seemed to evaporate. What I wanted more than anything was to fall asleep as Stephen had done, but this also seemed impossible. Instead, I fell into a hypnotic state that seemed to pacify my turmoil somewhat. It was calming, floating through nothingness and listening to my own heartbeat. It seemed to get louder and louder, and pulse through the water after so many hours — days? weeks? — in that suspended state.

I put my hand to my chest, noticing a peculiar rhythm in the pulsing sound. There was another little bump in the middle of the beats, almost imperceptible at first. It was like another heart was beating near me. Experimentally, I reached out and felt warmth.

Someone was here with me. My hand searched around and connected with another set of fingers. It sent a wave of comfort through me, and my fingers closed around the hand of whoever was with me in the dark. The hand grasped me back. My heart started to flutter—I already knew who it was. After all, we'd been here together before....

"Lea," I stammered. "It's you, isn't it?"

"Yeah."

My eyes ached with the threat of oncoming tears. My other hand searched for hers, and I found it. We held to each other. She was the only thing that I had in this world.

"God, Lea, why did you have to go?" I moaned, yet happier than I'd ever been. I didn't know how long I'd have with her, or if she was even real, but I felt peaceful. "You're half of me. We've been together since the beginning. I can't do this without you. I'm not strong enough."

"That's not true at all," her voice said. "We were each other's strength, but that doesn't mean we couldn't stand by ourselves."

"But everything's broken now. I'm not the same. Nothing's the same. I'm scared of everyone and everything. I'm scared to love anything. You have no idea what you did to me, what I've been through. I'm ruined."

"Sarah," she said and pulled me closer, holding tight.

"Lea, I need you. We're two parts of a whole, and you were always the better part of that. You were born first. I followed. Somehow in those few extra minutes, you gained all the wisdom I could never understand. You always had it and now I'm lost. I have no one to follow," I murmured, and felt her forehead press against mine.

"We were born together for a reason," she told me. "Our lives were beautiful, weren't they? But we were never half of a whole. No one is completed by another person. No one becomes happy that way. Happiness is something you have to chase after, and you have to have the courage to hold onto it, and the strength to weather the storm when it goes away for a while. But it'll always come back. It will always come. That part of your life is over, and my life is over for good. You can't hold on to an instant for the rest of your life. You can't stop halfway through. You've got to keep going."

For the third and final time in my life, I felt that ringing in my chest. Something deep inside of me broke loose and I held Lea tightly, hoping to hold her forever but aware that I couldn't.

The memories came to me. My first memory of life, being so small with her in our crib. I saw us at the seaside in silly big hats with plastic yellow buckets. We'd made sandcastles that day. I saw our backyard, and heard our shrill, innocent laughs. I saw birthday candles, and scraped knees, and Christmases, and first days of school with our hands clasped, holding onto one another for strength. The same strength that had come during thunderstorms, bad days, at the end of fights, and on the nights after break-ups. I felt her running beside me and our dog in the last light of the day, and felt her breathing beside me on the couch during the credits of so many movies. And I remembered, finally, the last day I'd seen her alive. She had come back from somewhere — spending time with friends, maybe, or perhaps Unreal City. I'd been short with her and when she'd gotten the text from Stephen to come and meet him, I'd said, "Well, don't disappear on me, again."

We clutched one another for as long as we could, saying the silent goodbye we'd never had the privilege of last time. I wanted to freeze this moment like I'd done before with Felix in my garden, but it wouldn't work. She really had told the truth.

A current rose up and pried us gently apart. I felt her break away from me, and the last thing I remember of her is her fingers still trying to grip mine as she was swept away forever. For a while longer I hovered there, mourning the loss of the most important person I'd ever known.

I hardly noticed when a shaft of light cut through the darkness.

20

I LOOKED UP to see something very like the opening of a well, only I was at the bottom of it. Swimming upward, I broke through the surface of the water and gasped in the cool, fresh air. Each lungful was like new life. Air had never tasted so sweet.

Seemingly hundreds of feet above my head at the top of the shaft was a circle of light with little black specks moving around it. I called up, my voice echoing off the stone. An indistinct noise answered me and my heart leapt. It could've been a voice.

After about a minute of treading water and trying to keep afloat, something was tossed down onto my head. It was a rope. My heart skipping with nearly painful delight, I grabbed hold of it with trembling hands and tugged. It seemed safe, so I began my difficult ascent. By the time I was halfway up, my shoulders and hands were screaming with pain, but I didn't care. There was a way out. I was going home.

Nearing the top I couldn't see the specks any longer, and I called up for help as I tried to hoist myself over the edge. I almost let go when Joy leaned down and caught my hand. I stared at her in shock as Angus grasped my other hand and I was pulled over the side onto solid ground. There stood Felix, purring, and next to him was a familiar I'd never seen before. It was shaped like a rabbit carved from ice. Aodh's face was in the trees behind us.

"Joy—how in the—what are you all doing here?"

Joy and Angus shared a relieved look. "I got worried about you when you didn't come back inside after a long time, so I went searching for you on the sea cliff. You were lying in the grass and Felix was there beside you. He told me everything. He told me what you did, and where you went—"

"—and how I couldn't follow you," Felix finished for her. "I figured you'd get yourself stuck down there, so I waited beside your body for her to show up. After she heard what you'd gotten yourself into, we just had to pray that you worked things out. I felt a shift happen. Felt my friend had finally been set free. So I called him to our side so that Joy could make the pact with him. There she sits, reborn," Felix added, gesturing with a flick of his tail to the rabbit at his side. She was beautiful and pure, and the surface of her glimmering skin was etched with beautiful symbols. Her eyes were like two pearls, shining with that miraculous opalescence of the familiar's life energy. I was speechless.

"It was easier the second time," Joy remarked when she saw the tears welling up in my eyes. "You know I couldn't have left you stuck down there."

"Joy, you—"

"I know. You don't have to say anything. I chose this life over the other. I chose the one with you alive and very much a part of it," Joy said, her brilliant smile lighting her face. I couldn't stop my tears from falling. I took her in my arms and as we embraced, I smiled at Angus.

"You brought her here, didn't you?"

"Taught her how to find you and everything. Don't worry. You can thank me later. You've got a true friend there, Sarah, and not too bad looking, either," he grinned, and she broke away from me to give him a shy grin.

Joy waved her hand and the well closed up, leaving only earth sprouting with shoots of new spring grass. "She's a natural," said the rabbit at her side. "I predict there will be a few peaceful decades for us, old friend." She looked over at Felix, who flashed his wicked grin.

"Some well-fed decades are all I hope for," he said, licking his lips and studying me like I was a Thanksgiving turkey.

As we sat in Joy's garden, I told them all that had happened down in the ground, and Joy was relieved to hear that Stephen's passing came by his own choice. With the oppressive danger dispersed, Joy decided to make a celebration of our remaining time in her garden. She commanded the flowers and grass to grow all around us until we wandered through forests of tulips, roses, hyacinths, narcissus, and bluebells. Angus, Aodh, Felix, Joy's new familiar and I followed her through endless antique stores crammed with all manner of nostalgic wonders, through recreations of the 1920s and the regency period. We feasted and flew and played among the clouds, and all too soon I found that my time in the garden was ending.

I floated back to Earth in a peaceful manner, feeling as if I'd been hollowed out—the good was gone along with the bad. When I awoke, I was shivering in the tall grass overlooking the sea. Joy was sleeping beside me, still exploring her section of Unreal City. I watched her for a long while in the gray light of those quiet moments before dawn, and when the sun rose in a blaze of orange and peach, I got to my feet. Felix was perched atop a stone cross at the edge of the cliff, and I waded through the grass to join him. I clung to the cross, smiling uncertainly. He smiled back.

My eyes turned to the sunrise over the waves, a view like liquid mercury in the light of the newborn day. I was still stunned by everything, overwhelmed and unable to start planning everything that was to come. My heart still fluttered to think that I'd spoken with my sister just hours ago. I'd gotten to say goodbye, to let her know how much I loved her and I missed her.

My hand went to my neck where the pendant that housed her ashes still hung. With numbed fingers, I clumsily undid the clasp from behind my neck and looked down at it. All that was left of her fit inside my palm. I closed my fingers around it, and with eyes squeezed shut, I tried to remember the warmth and light of the succession of memories that had blazed in my heart in the deepest part of Unreal City. To my surprise I felt a smile on my lips. My eyes opened again to the light of the sun. It was almost above the waves now.

In an almost involuntary action, my arm lifted high into the air, my hand tilted back and I took a deep breath. Then I hurled the pendant forward with all my might. I saw the light catch it in midair as it flew, and my chest clenched with a longing that wasn't quite regret. Seconds later, the necklace disappeared into the ocean.

I watched the place where it had sunk for a while. I stood there until the sun was over the sea, and jumped when cold fingers touched my shoulder. Joy was there, smiling cautiously at me. I returned the grin. She gave me a searching look, and I knew she wanted to ask what I was doing.

"Just...just saying goodbye," I said, putting my fingers to the space around my neck.

"Oh," she murmured, seeing the pendant was gone. She tilted her head. "Well, I could leave you here for a while, if you want a little more time to—"

"No," I said, taking a step away from the cliff. Felix leapt off the top of the cross to follow me. "I've had my moment. And no moment needs to last forever."

READ ON FOR A SPECIAL PREVIEW OF

THE ANGEL OF ELYDRIA

BOOK ONE OF
THE DAWN MIRROR CHRONICLES

A POWER TO UNLOCK THE PAST
BRINGS DANGER...AND DEATH

CHAPTER ONE

THE LAST MORNING

THROUGH THE HAZE of sleep, Penny knew that this particular dream was dangerous, though it began as any other dream might.

Penny wandered through a forest, searching for an eerie voice that called her name. She found herself at a lone apple tree that didn't belong in the sea of pines.

Dig…I've got to dig, *her dream-logic ordered.* The entrance is buried here. Someone once showed me how to get there, it was…

Penny dropped to her knees in front of the fruit tree.

The atmosphere changed. Her awareness became too clear—so much so that it seemed to sting her eyes. She was awake inside of her dream, but lacked any form of control. The vividness intensified to the point of agony and Penny tried to scream. Nothing came out. A violent gust of wind knocked her off her knees and onto the ground.

All at once an immovable pressure crushed her. Talons gripped her body as a great white heron swooped in front of her eyes. The bird's beak appeared crooked and malformed.

The heron drove its beak deep into her body with a mercilessness that paralyzed her, its knife-like bill drilling into her abdomen. Horror electrified Penny and she tried in vain to wriggle free. A burst of revulsion assaulted Penny when she realized that the massive bird was searching for something within her body. She was still unable scream but somehow felt no pain.

The bird grew still and with a swift yank withdrew from the wound, revealing an enormous black spider clamped in its beak. Eight spindly legs twitched and twisted in the air, probing for something to hang onto.

A deep, resonating voice split through Penny's panic. "I have removed it. Now you will be hidden no more."

This time Penny screamed and the clear, sharp sound drew her back into reality. She tumbled onto the hardwood floor amidst a shower of various fluffy pillows. Her eyes snapped open and Penny found herself face-to-face with the grin of a teddy-bear.

Penny sighed as she untangled herself from her homemade quilt and sat up. Grumbling, she ran her fingers through her tousled black hair and started to rearrange her bed, listening to the footsteps pounding up the hallway.

Penny's door flung open as her inquisitive mother popped in. "What's all the noise about?" Paulina asked, failing to sound nonchalant. Her long black hair was pulled back, hidden under the usual bandana. Her gray eyes flitted over Penny with concern.

"It was nothing—just had a weird dream, that's all," Penny told her with a yawn and her mother gasped with intrigue. Penny ignored her and moved to the closet to arrange the day's ensemble.

"A dream? Was it unusual?"

Penny scoffed a little under her breath and suppressed the urge to roll her eyes as she inspected a skirt from her bedroom floor, then tossed it aside. "It *was* pretty vivid actually, but—"

Penny was interrupted by an excited giggle from her mother. "Hold that thought—I'll go get the dream dictionary. It could be a sign! We've got to interpret it while the imagery is still fresh in your mind. Sit tight!" Her mother tramped back downstairs, muttering to herself.

Penny shook her head as she pulled a jacket and striped shirt from her closet and slunk to the bathroom. As she got dressed and brushed her teeth, her mother returned to lob question after question about her dream through the bathroom door. Penny slapped water onto her pale, heart-shaped face and smoothed her hair as she answered. Her wide blue eyes and youthful features suggested she was younger than her actual age of twenty.

"A spider, huh? It says you have a good chance of finding money or getting a letter from an old friend," Paulina muttered, her excitement palpable even through the closed door.

Penny tried to focus on her mother's words as she did her best to tame her short, wiry black hair. This was a familiar ritual with her mother. *At least she isn't trying to cast a spell to keep me safe from inauspicious omens today,* Penny thought before she opened the bathroom door.

"Lookin' good, kid," Paulina said in a chipper voice, looking over Penny's skinny, boyish frame swimming within her jacket. "Need me to drive you over to the college today?"

"No thanks, Maddie's picking me up," Penny said as she descended the stairs. It was a cozy house with just enough room to move around in. Penny much preferred it to the dingy apartment on the other side of town that they had occupied before. There was something charming about the sleepy little neighborhood where they'd settled.

"Oh well, I need to get to the shop anyway," Paulina sighed. "Remember, you've got to be there too right after class because my plane leaves around five and heaven knows I'm going to need extra time. I *know* I've forgotten something. I always forget something."

Penny stopped on her way to the kitchen. *Of course—Mom's going to see Grandma this weekend.* Penny shook her head, which still seemed to be filled with cotton, and scanned the counter to see if there were any muffins left. The kitchen smelled of exotic spices and sunlight poured in through the windowpanes, dappling the many aromatic herbs and flowers that her mother grew to sell in their store.

Penny grinned when she found a wealth of fresh muffins on the counter and plucked up her favorite—banana nut. She turned to leave, stopping when she noticed her mother collapsing into the chair beside the kitchen table, rubbing her temple.

"Is something wrong?" Penny asked, drawing closer. It wasn't at all like Paulina to react this way about seeing Penny's grandmother; she more often than not spoke of the woman with a kind of forced optimism.

"Oh, it's nothing. I've just had a little bit of a headache since I woke up…I think it might be a migraine coming on…" her mother mumbled.

Penny stood by her for a moment, bewildered. "A migraine?" she inquired, surprised. "You never get migraines."

Paulina shrugged. "Never too late to start, I guess—anyway, you'd better get outside. Madeline will be here any second and you don't want to keep her waiting."

"Well, don't work too hard. See you later." Penny waved to her mother, swept up her book bag that lay by the door, and slipped outside.

Penny grimaced upward as she took a bite out of her muffin. Gloomy blankets of deep gray clouds covered the Oregon sky and the humidity was palpable in the autumn air. She hummed as she took a seat on the curb in front of her house and stared at the whispering woods growing alongside the houses on Hillshire Lane. Her mind flashed to the image of a twitching mess of legs being extricated from her body cavity and a sick feeling washed over her.

As she sat waiting, Penny thought she sensed a peculiar heaviness pressing down from somewhere high in the sky, as if a huge balloon, filling with air, was threatening to pop. The wind whistled by and brought a flurry of burnt orange leaves with it. The nippy breeze succeeded in undoing any progress that Penny had made in arranging her hair.

Something feels really off today. Maybe all that prophetic dream junk she always talks about might actually mean something for once, Penny mused.

Heavy moisture clung to her cheek. The clouds were swollen with rainwater, and the only sound was the rattling of dead leaves blowing across the gravel. Penny shook her head again and smirked at herself.

Yeah, right. If anyone hangs around Mom enough they'll start looking for cosmic messages in alphabet soup. It was just a stupid dream; I shouldn't let it get to me. I've gotta cheer up—it's Friday, after all.

It was those insignificant moments she spent, sitting alone on the curb, which Penny would always think back on after the end of her life on Earth; the simple act of staring into the pines with her peace yet unbroken, while the wind raced onward to wherever it was destined to die.

THE QUIET OF morning was disturbed as a car glided around the corner and the chorus of an 80s rock song rang out through the neighborhood. Penny stood and waved to the driver as the car rolled up alongside her and stopped. She yanked open the door and jumped into the passenger seat, then lowered the volume with a brisk turn of the knob before looking over at Madeline.

"Glad to see you're cheerful as usual," Madeline said with equal parts mirth and annoyance, her pink star-shaped earrings swinging as she drove off. Madeline's wispy blonde hair hung around her shoulders and her blue eyes scanned the road, buried under vibrant pink eye shadow. She was a striking beauty and this often proved to be a source of insecurity for Penny.

"So, I think I'll be getting a solid B for today's essay. How'd yours turn out?" Penny asked, though she already had an idea what the answer might be.

Madeline gave a derisive laugh and turned the music back up. "I didn't even do it—practice ran late. Besides, Arlington is crazy if he thinks any normal person can handle this workload. Why do teachers always seem to think that we only have *one* class to keep up with?" she scoffed.

"He *is* kind of ridiculous, I'll admit, but all the same…you probably shouldn't just blow it off," Penny replied, her words transforming into a massive yawn.

Madeline shot her a look. "Let me guess. You stayed up all night again, didn't you? Please, *please* tell me you're not reading that girl-power detective series for the fourth time," she moaned.

"Fifth," Penny mumbled under her breath.

"Wow. You *still* haven't changed since the sixth grade," she teased.

Penny ignored her comment. For the rest of the drive, she listened and nodded as Madeline told her about all the praise her dance instructor had given her last night.

Twin Rivers Community College was a small, out-of-the-way school hidden among the overgrowth of trees that crowded the Oregon town. The buildings were dilapidated, weatherworn, and charmless.

Madeline parked and they made their way toward the campus, the biting chill on the wind carrying invisible droplets of rainwater. Halfway across the parking lot, Penny noticed Madeline stumbling and raised her eyebrows. Her friend's face had taken on a peaky color and her usual spunky nature seemed strained.

"You okay?" Penny asked.

"Yeah… I just started feeling a little messed up—bad headache. It's this drab weather," she said in a shaky voice and smiled, trying to recapture her usual level of energy.

Penny's brow furrowed. "My mom had a headache, too. I'll bet something's going around. Don't come near me, I can't get sick this close to midterms." She drew away from Madeline.

"I just hope I can make it through Arlington's class without falling asleep. As if it wasn't miserable enough already," Madeline sighed. They wove through the thin crowd of students shuffling their way to class, and drops of cold rain began to splash down.

"Argh! Let's hurry!" Penny exclaimed, using her book bag as an umbrella. They sped over the misty grounds until they reached the overhang outside their classroom and scurried indoors, dripping all the way over to their seats.

It was a cramped, square classroom with twenty or so desks crammed into it. A young man in the front row stared in a stupor at the words their professor scribbled onto the blackboard with chalk. A group of girls in the seats behind Penny shrieked with laughter at something on the screen of a cell phone they were passing around. Professor Arlington set the chalk down with a curt click and swiveled around to face the class. He was a willowy young man with soft, mousy brown hair that hung in an elegant curtain to his chin. A pair of round glasses were always sliding down his nose; Madeline sometimes kept a tally when she was particularly bored. Since he was skinny and rather tall, he had something of a stretched look about him. He clapped his hands together and peered around at the class with a half-smile.

"All right, everybody. I trust you've all been working long and hard on your papers, yes? Did anyone have a particularly exciting thesis they'd like to share?" he asked in his usual brisk tone, his hopeful smile fading when nobody so much as blinked an eye in response. Penny could almost feel Madeline's annoyance radiating off her.

Penny felt a little sorry for their professor—she had taken a liking to him and his optimistic efforts to teach literature to a group of people that had little to no interest in the subject. While Madeline classified him as 'intolerable', Penny harbored a quiet admiration for his enthusiasm. Yet with the unrelenting workload he assigned, she could understand why he was scorned by the majority of the students. Professor Arlington sighed before moving to collect the papers from the six or seven people who'd bothered to complete the assignment. Penny held her paper up as he walked by and Professor Arlington added it to the stack, and then halted, swiveling his head back to look at her. Penny felt a bit peeved at his apparent surprise; she was one of the few students who could be relied upon to complete every assignment. His pace slowed significantly, and Penny worried she'd fall asleep before he made it back to his desk.

At the front of the classroom, Professor Arlington turned and looked around the room. Penny watched him in a sleepy daze. Madeline's head was down on her desk and the rest of the class had already assumed their usual coma-like positions in anticipation of his lecture. The professor's eyes skimmed across Penny and he rubbed his forehead, his expression strained.

"Class...is dismissed," he said in a quiet voice.

Startled, Penny sat up and blinked in astonishment. He had never dismissed, let alone cancelled, a class before. Half of the class straightened up but stayed silent, now rapt with attention. Professor Arlington appeared even more uncomfortable when no one stirred.

"Did I misspeak? Class is dismissed!" he repeated with sharper enunciation, his face growing chalky.

"But—sir," a girl from the back spoke up. "We just got here—"

"I am quite aware of that, Miss Winslow. Please, all of you, leave."

In a state of befuddlement, the students started to pack up. Penny rose from her seat, took her book in hand and strode from the classroom with Madeline close beside.

"What was that all about?" Penny asked, still surprised. "Do you think he's mad no one did the essay?"

"Maybe he got sick, I don't know," Madeline said with disinterest.

"He didn't look sick, he looked upset," Penny insisted, reaching for her bag to prepare for another sprint through the drizzle. She stopped short. "Oh no—I left my bag!"

"Then go get it," Madeline said, exasperated. "I'm cold and my head hurts. Let's hurry up and get out of here."

Uneasy about intruding on her professor after he'd ordered them to leave, Penny plucked up her courage, doubled back, and cracked open the door. When she peeked inside, her heart all but stopped beating.

Through the crack in the door, Penny could see Professor Arlington standing at the back of the room, surrounded by thousands of tiny points of white-gold light that looked like bubbles floating in a glass of champagne. In shock she watched him move his hand along the empty space in front of him, drawing strange, silvery writing. The letters hung in mid-air, bleeding like ink from a fountain pen. They hovered for a moment, then pulsed with a bright flare and faded.

He waved his hand again and produced more silvery writing from thin air. The lettering looked to Penny like arcane runes, shimmering as bright as tinsel. Professor Arlington wore a tormented expression, as if enduring an inordinate amount of pain. The lights in the room flickered from a surge of energy that seemed to radiate from the center of the room. Trembling, Penny backed away and let the door slam, trying to remember how to breathe.

That—that wasn't real, I'm hallucinating, it's not possible... Penny's mind raced even faster than her heartbeat, and she felt an alarming rush of lightheadedness. She swiveled around and charged away from the classroom at full speed to where Madeline stood waiting for her. Penny splashed through the mud to her, adrenaline pumping through her veins.

"M-Maddie!" Penny choked out, her voice sounding foreign to her own ears. Madeline looked over, her expression telling Penny that she was in a sour mood. "I—I—"

"What happened?" Madeline asked, looking impatient.

"In there—he was—it was—I can't even explain," Penny said in a fluster, cursing herself for being unable to articulate what she had seen.

Madeline let out a long sigh. "Honestly, Penelope..." she hissed as she trudged past.

Realizing Madeline was heading to the classroom, Penny yelped out loud, unable to stop herself. "Maddie, no! Don't go in there, please!" she shouted and chased after her, her voice sounding high and unnatural. She ignored the sidelong glances she was getting from bystanders. "It's dangerous—please!" Her anxiety doubled.

Madeline flashed Penny an irate glare and marched into the classroom. Penny froze and felt the blood drain from her face as the door shut behind Madeline. Just as she forced her legs to unstick themselves and move forward to rescue her friend, Madeline exited the classroom.

With a nonchalant stride that Penny hadn't expected, Madeline joined her, Penny's bag in hand. Dumbfounded,

Penny's lips parted in disbelief as Madeline shoved Penny's bag at her and kept walking. With a little groan, she jolted after Madeline.

"Did—did you see it?" Penny asked in an unsure tone. "Did you see the…?" she trailed off, unable to find a word for what she had witnessed.

Madeline's brows arched in irritation. "Listen Penny, you don't have to pretend any more. I should've just gone with you. I know how anxious you can get…with your fainting spells and all."

Penny's frustration overwhelmed her. "I'm not making anything up! I saw something—something impossible in there! You've got to believe me, Maddie," she sputtered, her nerves jangling.

"What? What was so mind-blowing, hmm?" Madeline inquired, no longer concealing the annoyance in her voice.

Penny's expression darkened; if she tried to explain herself, she would sound insane. "It was—I don't know—why are you so mad all of a sudden?" She crossed her arms over her chest.

"I have a pounding headache, I'm soaked through, we drove out here for no reason because apparently Arlington is blossoming into a drama-queen, and you're trying to play some weird game that I'm really not in the mood for," Madeline shot back.

"You saw *nothing* out of the ordinary?" Penny demanded, growing defensive.

"Nope! Everything was perfectly fine. He even wished me a pleasant afternoon. Must be my lucky day." Madeline came to an abrupt halt as they stepped into the wet parking lot. "Now, do you want me to take you home or are you walking over to the shop?" she asked in a business-like tone.

Penny stared down at her worn gray low-tops and exhaled. "The shop…"

"Well, have fun at work. Bye." She waved a half-hearted goodbye to Penny and stalked away. Penny ran her fingers through her damp hair and shut her eyes, disturbed by the possibility that what she had seen could have been the product of an unsound mind.

ABOUT THE AUTHOR

A.R. Meyering is a graduate in English from the University of California Santa Barbara with a specialization in Victorian/Neo-Victorian Literature. She is the author of the steampunk-fantasy series 'The Dawn Mirror Chronicles.' She is also the author of a dark fantasy *Unreal City* which won quarterfinalist in the Amazon Breakthrough Novel Award contest and garnered a positive review from Publisher's Weekly. Her heart pounds for the horrifying, the sublime, the delicate, the elegant, and the fascinating. She is a life-long fan of fairytales, gothic horror-shows, clever mysteries, children's stories that aren't quite for children, steam-powered wonders, and sweeping fantasies. She is a dedicated geek and gamer, an educator, and pug enthusiast.